LANNEN'S LAND

By the same author

Hodder Goes Home
Hurlock's Law

LANNEN'S LAND

VANCE MACKENZIE

A Black Horse Western

ROBERT HALE · LONDON

ISBN 0 7090 5825 X

Robert Hale Limited
Clerkenwell House
Clerkenwell Green
London EC1R 0HT

Photoset in North Wales by
Derek Doyle & Associates, Mold, Clwyd.
Printed in Great Britain by
St Edmundsbury Press Ltd, Bury St Edmunds, Suffolk.
Bound by WBC Book Manufacturers Limited,
Bridgend, Mid-Glamorgan.

PROLOGUE

He died in Gerrard's Creek. They were waiting, slouched behind the rocks on the high ridge, and when he rode below, their Colts cracked and sent him whirring out of the saddle.

He was stone dead before he hit the ground. But that didn't stop the big, heavy one drilling two more slugs into the chest, just to make sure.

The flies were already buzzing round the body before the three men had mounted up, swelling themselves on the blood gushing from the gaping holes in the body, even before the three horses had begun to amble.

The men rode slow. There'd been no witnesses. They were in no hurry. The sun glistened on the sweat beads that bubbled on their foreheads. Even at nine o'clock in the morning it was too hot to hurry.

Though cursing the heat, they were feeling mighty pleased with themselves. They had done what they set out to do. They'd done it well. Already Ben Lannen was history.

Two of them carried on down the creek, the third, blocky in the saddle, peeled off to the left. 'I'm obliged to you,' was all he said.

After they'd gone the buzzards came, beating their wings violently as though in blood-lust, then gliding down to feed.

It would get much hotter.

ONE

Tom Lannen rode into Plainsville in mid-afternoon, a tall, slim figure in the saddle, sending up a cloud of dust to the blazing sky. He was known here – but lately not so well as his son. Ben had been by far the more sociable and business-like of the two of them. When there were transactions to be made, recently it had been the boy who'd been coming to town. Though not quite nineteen, his handshake had been as trusted as any man's.

Even in this heat and despite the drought, Plainsville seemed to Lannen far busier somehow than when he last visited. He'd heard it was fast expanding, on its way to becoming a big cow-town, and there were corrals, clusters of them, where once had been open grazing.

He continued at a pace down the narrow, winding main street which he'd known as a quagmire in rainy seasons gone by. After two years, though, with no more rain than one time might fall in a wet month, everywhere was now so dry a man needed to hide behind a wet bandanna just to cross the street. And still the dust would burn his eyes like sulphur as if he was traversing some badlands.

Lannen reined in before the jailhouse. He'd practically bust his back getting here – but as he dismounted it came to him there was no hurry. He climbed the two steps stiffly and slowly. He'd come to claim his son's body. Nothing he could do would bring him back.

Why rush? He wouldn't be leaving until he'd gotten some straight answers.

He stopped, took off his stetson to fan himself, revealing a head of close-cropped, iron-grey hair, and wiped the back of his neck. He was thinking about what he was going to say. A more hot-blooded man might in the circumstances have been running as wild as an unbroken stallion, but not Tom Lannen.

Tom Lannen would have his revenge on whoever killed his son, if it took him the rest of his life. There was nothing more certain in his mind. And he'd go about it at his own sure and methodical pace, so there would be no mistakes.

News had reached him, via Deputy Casey, about an hour ago, and he'd ridden straight in. He'd been up hazing a small jag of steers from a high and arid patch to a better graze down by the spring, knowing in his mind that something was wrong. Ben should have been back around noon. Some boys might have spent all day over the two or three purchases, but Ben had not been that type. He'd have come home directly even if there had not been urgent need for him to work on the farm – and there was always that.

And so Tom Lannen had sensed there was something wrong, even before the message had reached him, the message that a couple of drifters had come by the body in Gerrard's Creek, and brought it into town, looking to claim some reward for their services. All they'd got in the event was a lengthy interrogation from Sheriff Dale Danvers.

The two men had been allowed to depart, grumbling, to the Lafayette Saloon, only after having undertaken to stick around for a couple of days and, if need be, to take the sheriff back to the exact spot where they'd made their find.

'Tom ... I sure am sorry,' said Danvers, laying down his glass of whisky and standing up the moment he saw his visitor. 'I sure am powerful sorry.'

Lannen looked at the big man before him and gave a bleak stare. When he spoke it was in the slow, nasal drawl of the native Texan. 'Tell me what you know, Sheriff.'

Danvers rested his boot on the chair and pushed it over in Lannen's direction, but the farmer shook his head at the offer of a seat. 'I guess I prefer to listen on my feet,' he said.

The sheriff lowered his haunches on to the corner of his desk, took out a bag of makings and began to build himself a smoke. 'About noon, two drifters came in ... bringing in with them ... uh ... your son's body....'

He stopped to light up. Lannen looked with distaste at the whiskery stubble on his squat chin, the narrow-set eyes that bulged as he coughed when the smoke hit his lungs. He figured him in the old days for a grifter or a thimblerigger or even a bankrobber. These days he was a sheriff. The war had changed everything.

'Said they'd found ... it ... up by Gerrard's Creek, about an hour afore.'

'*Said* they found it?' Lannen repeated.

'Uh, yeah ... and I'm sure inclined to believe them, Tom.'

Lannen particularly resented being 'Tom'ed' by a man he'd met maybe three times, maybe four, and never on sociable matters.

'Why?'

The sheriff obviously found the directness of the question more than a little disconcerting. He puffed out his cheeks, letting the smoke trickle out slowly. 'Waal ... I cain't see they had any reason for killing him ... or for not speaking the truth.'

'Punks don't need a reason!'

'I never said they was punks,' Danvers interrupted, with a mild irritation. 'I said they was drifters.'

'And you take the word of a couple of drifters.'

'If they'd killed a man ... a boy ... they'd have been plumb stupid to bring him in.'

'So now you're telling me you've come upon two

drifters that are mighty honest ... *and* mighty
smart.'

The big man blew out a smoke ring and watched
it hover. 'They might not be too weighed down
with either quality, but I don't figure 'em for
cold-blooded killers – or for greenhorns!'

'What do you figure 'em for?'

'Plain ordinary drifters.'

It was the sheriff's turn to stare at Lannen. He
was beginning to understand why local folks had
always called Tom an ornery old cuss, and
preferred dealing with his son. 'Huh, how much
money d'you reckon Ben was carrying?'

'Not much. About ten dollars, no more than
that.'

'Well, it jest so happens he had ten dollars on
him when they brought him in.' He smiled thinly,
because he knew he was proving a point. 'So these
two here drifters sure ain't robbed him.' He
rubbed the stubble on his upper lip with a
forefinger. 'They cain't be all that bad.'

'I wanna see them,' said Lannen, without
returning the flicker of an expression. 'I wanna
hear their story. From them!'

Danvers puckered his lips and once more looked
the speaker up and down. Almost the first thing
he'd noticed about him when he walked in was
that he wasn't packing. This was mighty rare in
these parts, and hardly to be expected from a man
whose son had just been killed. This Lannen
didn't look a violent man, just a stubborn, mighty

humourless one. There could be no harm in him seeing the two men. Any father would want to do the same. As long as he, Sheriff Danvers, was there nothing could get out of hand.

'I sent 'em over to the Lafayette. We'll mosey across together.'

'It ain't necessary for you to go troubling yourself, Sheriff,' Lannen said levelly, 'you've already questioned them to your satisfaction, I take it.'

'I don't care how you take it, Tom,' Danvers said, equally flatly and raising his bulk off the desk. 'If you're fixing to see them, I'm going with you.'

This at least had drawn a trace of something like a pleasant smile from Lannen. 'I don't mean them any harm, Sheriff, just as long as I'm convinced they're what they say they are ... and had no part in it.'

'And suppose you figure different?'

Lannen smiled again, more enigmatically than before. 'There'd still be no trouble, Sheriff.'

Danvers quirked his grizzled eyebrows in amazement.

'Not till I've been back home and picked up an iron,' Lannen added.

The sheriff swung his dark face back to his desk and raised the glass of amber liquor that had stood there almost forgotten. 'I got me some mighty fine whisky,' he said, 'if you'd care for a shot before we go over there.'

Lannen shook his head. 'Let's go,' he said, impatiently. 'Drinkin' ain't in my nature at a time like this.'

'It'd sure get rid of some of that there edginess, Mr Lannen.'

He wondered for a moment why the sheriff had stopped first-naming him.

'Why, I'd like to be more edgy than I am,' he said. 'I wanna be more edgy than a green bronc in a thunderstorm till I've shot me whoever killed my son.'

TWO

Blake Kennedy was dealing blackjack when he saw Sheriff Danvers and another man walking over to his table.

He guessed the slim man with the sombre features and the ice-blue eyes must be the father of the boy they'd brought in. He was the spitting image of the corpse, only older and perhaps half a head taller.

'We've got company,' he said to the man opposite.

Carl Townend turned slowly and made a similar mental observation about the likeness of the man to the body they'd brought in. 'Looks like you've got some more business to chew over with us, Sheriff?' he said.

'This is Tom Lannen,' said Danvers. 'He's the one who's got something to say.'

'My name's Blake Kennedy and this here's Carl Townend. Ask away.'

There was something about the speaker's odd black eyes, set wide apart and staring out piercingly from a thin, hawkish face, that Lannen found disturbing somehow.

'Was my boy dead when you found him?'

'Yep,' said the flame-haired Townend, though the question had been directed towards his partner. He turned on Lannen his snubbed nose, square at the end like a pig's, and exposed his decaying teeth, in a mirthless grin. 'He sure was.'

'You figure he'd been dead long?'

Kennedy looked at Townend whose thumb and forefinger were round his cards, straightening their edges. 'I'd say a couple of hours, mebbe, wouldn't you, Blake?'

'At least.'

'And you found him about eleven o'clock, according to what you told the sheriff?'

'Yeah, it was exactly five after,' said Townend, drawing out of his vest-pocket a silver repeater, which he flourished to add authenticity. 'I checked the time.'

'That would mean he was killed about nine o'clock,' mused Lannen. If it were true it meant Ben had met his end within half an hour of leaving home – which figured because Gerrard's Creek was about thirty minutes' ride away. 'Nine o'clock's awful early in the morning for somebody to get killed.'

'When a body gits five or six slugs in it, it don't make no difference what time of day it be,' said Kennedy. 'He's dead.'

Townend was nodding seriously at that.

'You counted the bullet holes in him, did you?' asked Lannen.

Sheriff Danvers who had been staring out of the batwings gloomily, suddenly turned and scrutinized Kennedy.

'No ... I didn't count nuthin'. I just....'

'Five or six sounds about right to me,' put in Townend , quickly. 'He sure was peppered all over his chest.'

'C'mon Tom, let's go,' said Danvers. 'The number of bullet holes will come out in the doc's report.'

'I ain't finished yet,' said Lannen.

'And it seems to me you ain't got started yet,' said Townend, rising to his feet. 'It seems to me, mister, you ain't even begun to thank us for what we did.'

'Yeah,' agreed Kennedy, leeringly, 'we brought your son in. We could have left him there as buzzard bait. It seems to me you owe us a debt of gratitude.'

Lannen brought out a silver dollar and tossed it on the table. 'You're right boys,' he said, 'I'm forgetting myself. Have a drink.'

Townend glanced swiftly at Kennedy, sat down again and took up his cards, though not the silver dollar. 'Look Mr Lannen,' he said quietly, 'we're sure sorry about your son. All we did was find his body. We've told the sheriff all we know.'

'Yeah,' agreed the other one, 'all we know.'

'If you were in my position,' said Lannen, as if

as an afterthought, 'how would you go about establishing who killed your son?'

Townend looked perplexed. 'I ain't got no son.'

Kennedy evidently found that amusing. 'Me neither,' he smirked.

It was that which got Lannen mad, the joke at his expense, or his son's. But he fought to control his temper, knowing better. 'And I ain't got no other lead but you two boys,' he said. For a stretched second there was complete silence. 'That's why I gotta establish if you can help me.'

'You can establish what the hell you like,' thundered Townend, bringing down his fist heavily, scattering his own cards. His leathery features were taking on an even more florid shade. 'But keep us out of it. We're just passing through.'

'Not till you've answered my questions, you ain't,' said Lannen, matching the man's tone. 'You ain't goin' no place.'

Suddenly there was a scraping of chairs throughout the saloon, and the bar had cleared. Then another silence descended. Kennedy, grim-faced, lips tightly clamped, studied Lannen intently with his distempered eyes. 'That sounds like a threat, and we don't take threats, mister....'

'Sheriff,' said Townend, more agreeably, 'we don't have to answer none of this fool's questions, that right?'

Danvers nodded. 'He ain't the law. He cain't make you talk ... if you don't have a mind to.'

'And we ain't gonna,' replied Kennedy, picking up the iron man and tossing it back at Lannen. 'We ain't got nothing to say to this here fella ... who thinks 'cos he ain't carrying no gun he can fire off insults instead.'

'Don't worry,' Lannen retorted, 'next time we bump into each other, I'll be packing, all right.' He looked at the coin thoughtfully, and returned it to his pocket. 'I guess I'll be seein' you two gents again.'

Outside on the boardwalk, the sheriff put a restraining arm on Lannen's shoulder. 'Don't you reckon you're mebbe being a mite hard on those boys?' he said.

'Mebbe I am,' said Lannen, tersely, 'but like I says, they're my only lead.' He shot the sheriff a shrewd look. 'I had to get 'em all riled up to see what they're made of.'

'Hell, chances are they're what they say they are. And know no more about the shooting than you do.'

Lannen looked into the sheriff's eyes scornfully. 'Didn't you see their boots, Sheriff? They were real purty boots they was wearing. Those boys sure ain't tumbleweeds ... not rigged out like that, they ain't.'

'Jeez, you cain't go condemning men jest on account of what they got on their feet,' he said, staring at his own. 'They might jest have struck rich somewhere on the trail.'

'I ain't condemning them, Sheriff. I'm jest

saying they ain't what they say they are. They ain't drifters.' He didn't much like the way the townsfolk were standing around and staring at him. They didn't say anything – and they weren't about to do anything. They were just standing there. 'No drifter wears boots like that,' he continued, 'or if he does, they don't stay fancy for long. No drifter there's ever been turns down a silver dollar.'

'Bull,' snarled Danvers, 'this is all bull. You got it in your head these men are guilty, and you're trying to make everythin' fit.'

'And no drifter sports a silver timepiece like that fella was sporting.'

The sheriff spat morosely and ground the white glob into the dust with the sole of one of his own boots he'd gone back to staring at. 'Anybody who takes the law into his own hands in this town, ain't no friend of mine, Lannen.'

Lannen sighed. He'd gone from being Tom to Mr Lannen to Lannen in a half-hour, but that was the way he wanted it. 'I sure hope I don't have to take the law on myself. I sure hope you're gonna find whoever killed my son.'

'I'll ... uh ... speak to those two again, if it'll make you feel happier.'

'Yeah, you do that Sheriff. Ask them exactly why they bothered to bring a body into town. They don't look to me like the kind who'd want to go far out of their way to get involved with helping the law.'

Danvers gave a grudging nod. He had to admit there was something in what Lannen was saying. It would have been out of character for two such as that to commit any kind of public-spirited act at all, least of all one that would expose them to an awful lot of questions and attention.

What would have been more in character for a couple of drifters would have been to take Ben Lannen's ten dollars – and keep rolling. But then if their boots were as mighty pretty as Lannen had said, could be they weren't in urgent need of a few bucks. This, anyway, was the argument he thought about putting to Lannen – but the obdurate look on the farmer's face convinced him it would achieve nothing.

'Leave this to me, Tom,' he said sternly. 'Let me do the thinking.'

Lannen smiled a sad, thin smile at a private thought. 'Sure,' he said, when their eyes met, 'but there's times when thinking jest ain't enough. And this is one of them. I gotta have action, Sheriff.'

As his voice trailed off, he felt another great stabbing sadness in his heart. If only he had been in the habit of going to town on a Monday morning, rather than Ben.

THREE

When Lannen walked into Doc Harvey's surgery he had an awful feeling that Ben's body must be stretched out in the next room.

As if to confirm it, the doc's first words were, 'Tom ... I'd sure be obliged if you could wait to see your son when he's been ... uh ... cleaned up some.'

Lannen bit his lip and shook the hand that had been thrust out. 'Doc, I gotta see him now,' he said. 'I ain't expecting my son to be laid out all neat and tidy. I guess you're a doctor not an undertaker.'

He felt a shudder rack his body as he was shown in back. He'd seen dead bodies before, by the thousand, during the war. Corpses, many of them of boys even younger than Ben if the truth were known, had littered the field in half a dozen battles he'd been in. Nothing could be worse, he had always told himself, than that day at Cold Harbour. That scorching day in the June of '64. So much blood had been spilled on that day that anyone who survived it must ever look on death with the unflinching eyes of a butcher, he had always believed.

But this was different. This was his own flesh. A boy who'd been senselessly gunned down, denied even the right to defend himself.

There were weights on Ben's eyes and he was wearing a thin cotton shift. The boy's rigid immobility spoke for itself. Lannen smoothed back his son's dark hair away from his forehead and kissed the cold, taut skin. He continued to stare for a long time, a softness on his lean features that would vanish, perhaps for ever, the moment he left the room.

Then he left.

Doc Harvey was sitting at his desk, doing nothing except staring into space. He looked much older, Lannen judged, than when he'd last seen him, a year or two back. His floppy grey hair no longer looked right for the thin, beaky face. His eyes and cheeks had become pinched. In truth it was a face which looked nearer death than that of the corpse he'd just seen.

'I gotta ask you a couple of questions, Doc.'

The smile returned was only faint but enough to break the gravity of the medical man's expression as he motioned Lannen to a seat.

'There's not much I can tell you before I've sent my report to Danvers, I'm afraid.' He gave a dry, wheezing cough. 'It's this goddamn drought,' he said, fisting his chest. 'It's drying me up.'

'Uh ... Danvers?' Lannen prompted.

'He's gotta be the first to know all the details, you see.'

'Yeah, I understand that, Doc. But you can surely let me know how many bullets you ... dug out?'

Doc Harvey steepled his fingers and wheezed again.

'Yeah, there can't be any harm in that, Tom. There were five bullets, big ones, .45s, all from Colts, I should say.'

'Five bullets,' Lannen repeated, in a daze. 'My God, five bullets!'

So Kennedy and Townend had been right, but it was a shock to have it confirmed.

'And they were all in the chest.' The doc stopped and went to the window. 'Tom, if it's any consolation to you, I think I can safely say death would have been more or less instantaneous with that many bullets.'

Lannen grimaced. When he spoke, it came out as barely a whisper. 'One thing, Doc: is there any way of telling how many guns fired those five bullets?'

Doc Harvey turned from the window as though surprised by the question. 'Why, not exactly, Tom.' He fingered his frail chin thoughtfully. 'Like I say they were all the same calibre ... but there is one thing.'

Lannen felt himself rising from his seat, desperate for anything, any little thing at all, that might tell him something. He found himself nodding promptingly and wishing he'd retained his seat because his action seemed to have given the doc pause.

'Look, I shouldn't be telling you this, you know, not in advance of the report.'

'Doc, whatever you tell me, I'll sure ... uh ... keep it kinda private.'

Doc Harvey let out a slow, wheezing sigh. 'The bullets appear to be of two kinds. There were three of the usual nickel colour....'

'And the other two?'

'They were much darker. They were black in fact. I'd guess made of a different alloy. I've never seen any that colour.'

'Could be there were only two gunmen, then?'

'That I can't say. I'd guess – and it is only a guess – that the two black bullets came from the same gun.'

Lannen nodded. 'That figures.'

'But the other three, well, they could have come from three guns, or one. Or even two, for that matter.'

Lannen had a feeling the doc would like to tell him more, but was wary of it. He sat there, apparently deep in thought, giving the old man the opportunity to speak if he was going to.

'There was one other thing ... uh ... I think might help you, Tom.'

Lannen smiled thinly and prayed the doc wasn't going to get second thoughts.

'These black bullets went very deep. Fired at point-blank range, I should say.'

'And the others?'

'Not nearly so deep. And ... uh, as far as I can tell they were fired from high ground.'

Lannen's eyebrows shot up at this.

'You see, Tom, they were angled down, their tips pointing towards the sternum.'

'So you're saying, Doc, Ben was probably shot off his horse by somebody above him, firing three bullets. Mebbe from one gun, mebbe from more? Then somebody else came and stood over him and finished him off?'

The doc shifted uneasily. 'That's about it, Tom,' he said, after a moment's thought.

'Thanks, Doc,' said Lannen, putting his stetson back on and settling it. 'You've been mighty helpful.'

'Uh, you won't forget, will you, Tom, to keep it to yourself – what I've told you?'

'Sure Doc. I never forget a thing.'

Danvers returned to the jailhouse a thoughtful man. He broke open another bottle, shooting his deputy a suspicious glance, like he believed the last bottle had contained more than nothing last time he'd seen it.

But Len Casey, tall and lean with a handsome devil-may-care face grinned back. 'I've a notion old Tom Lannen's gonna stir up a whole heap of trouble, unless he finds out who killed his son.'

The sheriff nodded morosely. He had no doubt Lannen had been right. He should be seen to be leaning heavily on the two men. 'Lannen's an honest man,' he said, breaking off to take a swig from the bottle. 'He's got a reputation for it. He ain't gonna step outside the law.'

'He ain't,' replied Casey, staring at his boss quizzically, 'unless he has to.'

This was no doubt a reference to his handling of Kennedy and Townend. He should have been a deal more snippety with them. He could still be so. But he knew in his heart he wasn't going to be.

Much better if they were allowed – or encouraged – to move on. Better. He took another long pull, contorting his face like it was medicine. Better, all right. Neater all round. That way it all became somebody else's problem.

He didn't want anything more to do with them. He was getting too old to go wrangling with trouble. He took another powerful swig and wiped the perspiration from the back of his neck. Besides it was too damned hot.

'You let me worry 'bout that,' he said, throwing across a bad-tempered look. 'When I want your advice, I'll ask for it.'

Len Casey's eyes remained level. Then one of them closed, and he grinned.

FOUR

The milker was howling in pain when Lannen got back to Clearsprings Farm. He led her gently along the fence and into the barn.

As if knowing the way the animal waddled into the stall and stood there waiting, still howling.

He fetched the pail and set to work, his fingers barely having to squeeze the distended udders for them to yield milk. It was the job Mary used to do when they first moved into the farm. She'd only stopped doing it right at the very end when her strength had deserted her.

Recently Ben had done it. Now Lannen had lost his wife and son, he would be doing it himself.

Then he attended his horse, which he'd over-ridden on his way to town. While the big brown drank from the trough, he went round scattering meal for the chickens which had a roost in a corner of the barn. Finally, he turned the cow out for the night and carried the sweet-smelling pail into the house.

Soon he had the fire going and his dinner on the

stove. Even though he had no appetite, he forced a scant meal down. He was determined not to undermine his strength in any way, with the biggest, most compelling business of his life still to be done – and done soon if it was to be done at all.

Then he went to an old chest in back and brought out a sackcloth bundle. He stared at the wide-brimmed, grey cavalry hat that emerged, the gold tassel on the crown proclaiming it as having been worn by an officer. He rammed it back, his hand searching for a hard object.

The next item out was a small, one-shot derringer that he also tossed back, this time with disdain. Then he found what he was looking for, his Colt; and a moment later he laid hands on the tooled leather holster. It had been a long time since he'd worn it, the last occasion being at the second battle of Gettysburg when he was captured. He'd been in the Texas Cavalry, and a deadly shot. He whipped out the gun, his reflexes still like lightning. But it was the accuracy of his aim, with small arms or rifle, that had always amazed others.

During the war he'd killed and killed again, killed because there'd been no other choice. After Gettysburg he'd sweated out the rest of the war in the notorious Yankee prison camps, dreaming of only one thing ... getting back home to Mary and the farm, and vowing to himself he'd never kill again.

He'd never kill again, not after the blood he'd seen shed, the bloodshed he'd personally caused with his deadly aim that had grown to seem like a curse. When he returned home, he no longer dreamed of liberty; his dreams, engulfed in blood, had turned to nightmares. And he'd vowed, solemnly, that never again would he take another man's life, nothing could make him.

But now times had changed.

Lannen rose slowly from his reverie. For a few moments he had been back once again fighting for the eleven states, amid the carnage. He shuddered and went to the door to take in some clean air.

On most nights at this time he would do the same and take a survey of his land. Normally Ben would have been with him and they'd be talking about what had to be done next day.

It was the first time in a long while, since Mary had passed away in fact, that Lannen did not look out with a degree of pride.

On the west side was a slope of timber, much thinner now than it had been on account of its having provided the material for the cabin and its extensions, the barn and the fencing. To the east, and stretching round the back of the house, was the grazing for his cattle, of which he now had fifty head of Herefordshires. A very small herd, and not of the new fashionable Texas Longhorn, but it was all his and paid for.

To the south was his pot of gold. It was

practically the only thing on the farm that he hadn't put there or changed. It was a spring well, which had never failed. Always a plentiful supply of water eddied up from it and, even in the drought, it formed a good big pond.

It was on account of the spring that he'd set himself down here in the first place, before the war. And it was on account of it he'd called his land Clearsprings.

Other men, in times gone by, had gone for flatter and lusher plains, bigger spreads, greater proximity to town, because here at the northern end of the Territory water had never been seen as a problem. But those same men, or those who had followed them, had suffered heavy losses in stock and grass these last two arid years. Lannen's land alone remained unaffected because of his spring.

Spring or not, the two long years had been a hard, backbreaking struggle, but one which he'd begun recently to think he was winning. Certainly before the drought he had expectations of his herd doubling, and even now with the natural moisture of his lands he did not foresee losses in this time of almost universal pessimism. With Ben by his side, he would probably have had to think about taking on a hand some time in the next few years, if things had worked out. But on his own there was no way he could even run the place, let alone talk of expansion.

Now, however, there was no way he could afford to take anyone on – even if he thought he could find a suitable person. And what man would work on a farm like a son would work? True, there would be no shortage of offers if it were known he was setting on. Texas, in the grip of reconstruction, was positively overflowing with drifting cowpunchers looking for work. Except that work was not what many of them were really after. Killing and shooting, rustling and land-grabbing, this was more the order of the day. It was happening all over the place.

There was very little that either big stockmen or smallholders like Lannen could do against determined bodies of such men. The best that could be hoped for was to keep well clear. The law provided no relief. The Territory was full of lawmen appointed by the Yankee administration and most of them only there for what they could get.

Whether Danvers was one of those Lannen had no idea, but certainly the new sheriff was no Texas man. He'd suddenly appeared a couple of years back and somehow walked into the job. No doubt it had been reserved for him by some carpetbagging politician. With a sense of sheer frustration, Lannen pounded his right wrist into his left palm.

In a second, he was morose no longer. He could not afford the inactivity that went with such a mood. He was bounding to a cupboard, breaking open a box of slugs and feverishly thumbing them into his Colt. When a man wears a gun, it had

better be a loaded gun – and he'd heard the sound
of galloping hooves. Two horses, he judged.

Yesterday he'd have been walking out to see
who was paying him a visit, in spite of the
lateness of the hour. Tonight, however, he was
taking cover behind the window, pistol drawn, the
thought strong in his mind that whoever killed
Ben may just figure it in their interests to come
and kill him. They might have got to thinking that
unless they did so, if not today then tomorrow or
pretty soon thereafter, their own days were
numbered.

'Tom Lannen!'

He heard his name being yelled across the still
night air.

'Tom … you there? This is Thad Barnes.'

Lannen relaxed instantly, struck a lucifer to
light the lamp and then threw open the door.
'C'mon in, Thad,' he said, seeing the heavily-built
man dismounting. He noticed his daughter Betty
was with him.

'Tom … I've jest heard,' said Barnes, throwing
an arm round Lannen's shoulder. 'I've been outa
town all day. I just had to come right over the
moment I heard … and, well, see if I can do
anything to help.'

The possessor of the flat-crowned hat, white silk
shirt, grey coat and trousers and shiny black
half-length boots standing in front of him was not
a local man, either. He'd come down from the
north with a whole heap of new ideas, mostly

about how to make a fast buck, and no real
practical knowledge of cattle-rearing. But Lannen
had always had time for him. Barnes had been
quick to ask and quick to learn and, yes, quick to
make money, judging by the way he spent it.
What's more he'd always paid Lannen a fair price
for his cattle, thus saving him the long drive with
it up to Kansas.

Lannen nodded appreciatively. 'That's real kind
of you, Thad,' he returned.

'Anything at all, Mr Lannen,' said Betty. 'We'd
be more than willing to send a hand over for a day
or two wouldn't we, Daddy?'

Lannen's eyes flickered over her, taking in her
clear skin, the wide black eyes and the raven curls
that wreathed her face that was small and
girl-like in all its features. She was used to having
men stare at her and the fact that Lannen so soon
dropped his gaze told her he was a shy man, or at
least he was shy where women were concerned.

She was nodding promptingly at her father.

'Uh, yeah, we could spare a man for a couple of
days if … uh … it would help, some.'

Lannen looked from Thad to his daughter's
kind, earnest face, then back again to the man.
'That's mighty neighbourly of you,' he said. 'But I
reckon I'll … uh … manage.'

Barnes sat down stiffly on a bench and gestured
to Betty to do the same. Lannen judged there was
a slight awkwardness between them, as though
there was some reluctance on her part to be there.

Yet this did not square with the considerate look she'd lately given him – and she'd always appeared to him to be a kindly sort, not at all the type to resent paying such a visit, as an inconvenience or waste of time.

Time was, in fact, when it had crossed his mind what a fine match she might make for Ben – but he'd dismissed the fancy, figuring if there was quite a difference in a couple's ages, it ought to be the man who was the elder.

So what was it, Lannen wondered, that was dividing father and daughter?

FIVE

'Look Tom, I know this ain't really the time for this,' said Barnes, shifting his heavy frame awkwardly, 'but it might kinda reassure you to know if you want to get out now....' He coughed. 'I mean now you're on your own ... well ... I'd sure give you a good price for this place.'

Lannen massaged his chin, now in need of a shave, with his right hand. 'That's kind,' he said, 'but like I said last time you offered to buy me out, Thad, well I built this place, set down my roots here ... and now I reckon I'll be here to the finish.'

'The finish?' It had come from Betty, almost startled, though she tacked a slight laugh on to it, to cover her own embarrassment at her reaction.

'Yeah, the rest of my born days, ma'am.'

From the folds of his jacket Barnes suddenly produced a bottle of whisky and passed it over with a twinkle in his eye.

'That's real good stuff,' he said. 'It's McQuaid's, real Scotch whisky. I got a case of it shipped in. I figure you could use a drop of that right now, Tom.'

Lannen thanked him and set it down. He had no inclination to open it. He mostly only ever drank whisky when he was happy – and generally if he had enough of it, it turned him sad. Since Mary died he'd never been happy in his heart and thus seldom touched the stuff.

'Thanks,' he said again, because Barnes was looking at him expectantly, hoping no doubt for a taste of it himself. 'It looks mighty fine whisky.'

'Uh, Daddy's getting expensive tastes these days,' said Betty, smilingly taking her father's arm. 'Seems like just about everything we get these days has got to be freighted in. I keep tellin' him stuff ain't no wise better 'cos it's got a shipper's label on it. And it costs a deal more.'

Barnes was still looking expectantly. 'That ain't rot-gut, Tom,' he added, 'that's the real business. Had it brought up from Velasco.'

A drinking-man's face was Barnes's all right, Lannen was thinking, noticing the network of thin purple veins that spread across the massive jowls. His features were as blunt and craggy as his daughter's were finely sculpted.

Relenting, he got up and fetched two glasses, filling one which he handed to the smiling Barnes, and taking no more than two fingers for himself.

Barnes took a good pull and seemed to visibly relax. 'Tom,' he said, uttering the single syllable in an almost tender tone, 'Tom, I don't wanna push you right now, but I gotta tell you I think you're making one big mistake. A man on his own can't run this place.'

'I'll take on a hand in time, mebbe.'

Barnes looked doubtful, started pulling at one of the huge, grey side-whiskers that spread across the jowls. 'I could sure make use of this land, Tom. I could turn this into a mighty fine spread. I've got the money to develop it. And if you don't mind me venturin' it, I've got ... well, the will-power and the drive to make things happen round here.'

Lannen shrugged off the implied criticism of his own lack of either. 'Yeah, yeah,' he said, 'we've been over all this before. I know you think I'm jest a small-time homesteader without ambition but, well, that's how I like to be.'

Barnes laughed. 'Tom, that's not what I think at all.' He took another gulp of his expensive whisky. 'But a man's gotta move with the times. Things are changin' fast. There's big money to be made in cattle. In longhorns like I got. That's what the market wants these days.'

'I've always had Herefordshires,' said Lannen, stubbornly. 'I kinda like the breed. I understand 'em.'

Barnes again spread his lips with mirth, then became suddenly serious. It was an alarming change of mood and it gave Lannen an uneasy feeling.

'Tom, I can't deny I need your water pretty bad. With it, I can sure turn me into one of these Texas cattle kings I hear so much about these days.'

Barnes stood up and helped himself to another

tumblerful. 'Why, we're right slap bang in the
middle of it all, here.'

There was a gleam in his eye as he spoke, but a
frustration was edging into his voice. 'We're
squarely on the trail of the big herds driving up to
the Kansas railheads. They'll take as much beef
as we can get up there.' He waved his free hand,
evidently in a northern direction. 'Them big cities
have got big appetites and they're pushing up the
price all the time. Tom, I can get me ten times
more per head than a couple of years back ... '

'Daddy ... ' put in Betty, gaining for herself a
thunderous parental glare.

'With your water I can keep on doubling,
trebling my herd, every year.'

'C'mon Daddy,' Betty said softly, 'I told you it
wasn't right to trouble Mr Lannen with talk of
business tonight. Let's go and give the poor man
some peace.'

'No, wait a minute, Betty,' Barnes said, the
anger of his earlier look now having turned to
something like despair. 'I jest gotta make Tom my
best offer ... now that we've got started on the
subject.'

Both Betty and Lannen had stood up but
Barnes remained solidly still.

'Listen, Tom, just listen to this. You sell out to
me, you get to live in this here cabin ... and I give
you a job for life and all found.'

Lannen was rocking slightly on his heels,
thinking about the offer. It was a good one all

right. It would certainly take a whole load of
weight off his shoulders. It would mean he'd never
have to bother his mind again about a thousand
things that running your own place entailed. The
work, too, would in most ways be a lot easier.
When a man hires himself out, he does no more
than his due; when he works for himself, he does
everything.

Barnes was looking at him expectantly. There
was a look of something like pity on Betty's
countenance.

Finally Lannen broke the silence. 'Hell, cow-
punchin' on another man's land ain't for me,' he
said, his words almost stifled by Barnes's groan.
'At my time of life I jest ain't got the stomach for
takin' another man's orders.'

Barnes sprang up with remarkable agility and
stood toe to toe with Lannen, clapping his two
hands on the other's shoulders. 'Tom ... Tom ...
Tom. Listen to me. You wouldn't be takin' no
orders. You'd be giving them. I'll make you my
bossman. You'll be out there on the trail, your own
man, driving my herds all the way to Abilene.
Tom, I sure need someone I can trust, when
there's so much money at stake. Why, I'm hearing
all the time of trail-bosses who never come back.
They jest sell off the cattle and blow.'

He was tempted all right; once again he
experienced the strange urge to throw it all in. It
would be a new beginning, a challenge. It was his
turn to feel the need for strong liquor. Perhaps

sensing it, Betty was filling his glass and handing it to him, as he slumped down.

Ten minutes went by, maybe more. Lannen stared ruminatively at the floor, his face eventually becoming almost fierce with concentration.

'You know, Thad,' he said at last, 'once in the old days I drove a herd clear across Texas to Galveston. I guess in those days the cattle used to be going south, not north. I don't know.' He gave a shrug and swallowed some whisky.

Barnes was nodding. To him it seemed like Lannen was maybe sketching out his qualifications for the job he'd been offered.

'It was mighty warm work,' he continued. 'Most of all I remember the heat and the dust – a big herd will send up a cloud of dust a mile high – and the infernal pain in the....' He suddenly broke off to dart Betty an apologetic glance. 'Pardon me, ma'am. But, well, the truth is most times at night when a man gets off his horse he's so mighty stiff, he can't hardly stand up – yet he's so mighty sore he can't bear to sit down.'

It came to him that the unwonted drinking was beginning to loosen his tongue.

'And all the time I was away, d'you know what I was athinking? I was thinking about here, back home. And every inch of the trail I was lookin' over my shoulder at the thievin', the rustlin', the brawlin' going on and all. That ain't for me, Mr Barnes. Besides, I had my fill of movin' around during the war.'

Barnes stood up abruptly and snorted a look that Lannen calculated to be of pure disgust. 'I can see there ain't no talkin' sense into you,' he bawled, advancing to the door.

Then, surprisingly the big man stopped hesitantly, turned and shared a look with Betty, opening his palms, and scooping his eyes heavenwards, almost the actions of a patient and long-suffering man. It came to Lannen that that's what he, Barnes, really thought of himself. He'd made a very good offer. It had been refused. And he genuinely couldn't understand it.

'Daddy,' she said, a near whisper, 'I did tell you it ain't the time to be talkin' like this to Mr Lannen, after what's happened to him.'

Barnes advanced a step or two back into the room, making Lannen wonder if there was to be yet one more appeal. 'Yeah, you're right, Betty,' he said, 'you're always right. I don't know why I don't listen to you.' He swivelled in Lannen's direction. 'I sure am sorry, Tom. Uh, I was determined not to even mention farming matters.' He forced a tight laugh. 'This little lady surely drummed it into me enough before we came. But I guess my tongue ran away with itself … as it usually does.'

With that he turned on his heels.

'I gotta apologize for my daddy,' said Betty, giving Lannen a searching glance, as though trying to work out whether he'd been hurt by the conversation. 'He's hot-tempered at times, but he's a good man.'

'I know that, Betty.'

'That's why I insisted on coming to stop him talking like this but he wouldn't be told.'

'You don't need to fret none,' he replied. I know your pappy means well. It's a good offer. A damn good offer. And if I weren't such an ornery cuss, I'd take it.'

Her face was clouding. 'Not that I only came to keep control of daddy, you understand! I also wanted to give you my condolences.'

'Just promise me one thing, Tom.' They both swung round because Barnes had returned and was filling the doorway.

Lannen's eyebrows climbed.

'Just assure me you're gonna tell Zoot Hender the same as you're tellin' me. I gotta know you ain't gonna go selling out to him, now.'

Lannen wasn't smiling this time. 'Thad,' he said grimly, 'you don't need to ask that. I've told you I ain't selling and that should be enough.'

'Yeah, I know, Tom, but, well, that Hender he's kinda pushy. And not above resorting to a whole heap of low-down tricks to get his own way.'

'He made me his final offer only last month,' said Lannen, thoughtfully. In fact Hender had made so many final offers Lannen had run out of patience this last time. 'I don't reckon he'll be back again. I kinda bawled him out this time. It was none too purty.'

Barnes's heavy features screwed up at this. Lannen had also got to thinking.

SIX

Lannen was patching his fence bright and early next morning, getting all his jobs done before going into town, when noise and dust heralded the arrival of a group of fast-riding men.

He straightened up and counted five of them, coming over the swale, the black-coated figure of Zoot Hender at the head of them.

He was a man of about sixty who for some reason that nobody had ever been able properly to discover always wore a coat and pants, boots and gloves blacker than an old black oak – and his temper was as knotty as any tree of that species that Lannen had ever seen. Some did say he'd been in mourning for more than thirty years, since the day his wife, coming overland to join him, had been violated and killed by a Sioux. But it might have been no more than a rumour.

He reined in his black horse and flung himself out of his saddle, with surprising agility for a bulky man of his years.

'Tom,' he said, breathlessly, 'I gotta speak to

you.' He held up his gloved hand as if to stifle an expected objection. 'I was out of order last time we spoke and I wanna apologize.'

Lannen wiped his hands on his denim pants and narrowed his eyes. 'All right, Zoot, you'd better come in.'

He led the way in and slapped two more glasses on the table. He figured these Texas 'cattle kings' kind of expected nothing less.

Strangely, however, the sight of whisky seemed to be offending Hender. The smile which had been forming on his leathery face was turning into a sneer. Lannen suddenly realized the mistake he'd made as he followed the man's eyes to the red and yellow McQuaid's label.

'So Barnes has beaten me to it!' he snapped. 'I see he's left one of his fancy whiskies that he tries to impress folks with.'

'Uh ... he called last night.'

Hender snorterd so violently it seemed like he was about to explode. 'Only a rat of the first order, like Barnes, would call on a man on the day his son got murdered.'

'You prefer to leave it until the day after?'

With an obvious effort of will, which set deep lines on his brow, Hender remained calm. 'I've only come to offer my extreme condolences, Tom. Believe me, I'm truly sorry to hear about Ben. He was a fine young man, one that any father would have been proud of.'

'Thanks,' said Lannen, not unpleasantly. He'd

no wish at this stage to betray the suspicions crowding in upon him, and which after all were no more than merely that: suspicions.

Outside were four men. Here was a fifth. And there'd been five bullets in his son's heart! It could all fit.

'And being a charitable man,' Lannen went on, doing his best to disguise the sarcasm, 'I wouldn't have expected anything less from you – or from Thad Barnes, for that matter.'

'He came to try to buy you out – am I right?'

'That *was* mentioned,' said Lannen, taking a small sip of whisky that he didn't want. 'And I reckon you're just about to do the same – am *I* right?'

Hender stared at his glass, as though agonizing over whether he could bring himself to drink Barnes's liquor. 'If he's made you an offer, don't believe it. He's going bust! Everybody knows he spends twice what he earns. He'd go back on any deal as soon as he'd taken over your place.'

Lannen picked up his glass, very pointedly this time, and swirled its contents round the rim. 'He appears to me to be doing pretty well for himself. This is a mighty mature beverage he's shipping in.'

'Let me tell you about him,' said Hender, losing the battle with himself and tilting his glass to his lips. 'He's durned near overstocked himself out of existence. His grass has all but gone. A lot of his stock have died after eating poison weed –

because they couldn't find nuthin' else to eat. He's been forcing the pace and now he's paying the penalty. He'll stop at nuthin' to get your land. And I mean that! Your water is the only thing that can save him.'

Lannen smiled bleakly, thinking Barnes had said pretty much the same about his great rival. Who did he believe? Both men were desperate. There was no doubt about that.

If Barnes had been overstocking, Hender would have been doing the same – Lannen would have laid a tithe of his own land on it – such was the bitterly intense rivalry between them.

The look of livid anger that the whisky seemed to be putting on Hender's face couldn't help but bring Barnes's words back to him: 'He's not above resorting to a whole heap of low-down tricks to get his own way.'

Surely, murder, the murder of a young kid, couldn't be one of them? This was the thought that had kept him awake most of the night.

'How's *your* stock, Zoot?'

'I ... uh ... can't deny they'd be a sight healthier if I had that spring of yours seeping into my land, making the grass grow – even in a drought.' He took out his kerchief and rubbed it round the back of his neck, finally wiping his hands with it. He produced a black cheroot, but did not offer to light it, preferring instead to lapse into a gloomy silence.

'But I'll tell you this,' he said at last, 'my herd's

in a powerful better condition, thank God, than that up at the Bar X.' He jerked the cheroot in the vague direction of Barnes's ranch, and reminded of it, lit it. Only when the smoke had grown into a curtain between them did he proceed. 'Hell, Tom, I were runnin' cattle on this here range long before that fella was born. You know that, Tom, you're a man from these parts.'

Lannen nodded, without knowing entirely with what he was agreeing.

Suddenly, Hender was smiling to himself. 'Let me tell you this, boy, Thad Barnes hadn't been here three weeks before he sends for me.' He took another deep lungful, then blew out the smoke in Lannen's direction. 'He'd got himself a fat young heifer, struggling with its first calf. You know the kind, Tom, one of those too big for calving.'

Lannen nodded again, and poured his guest another slug.

'Well, it was lying there, breathing hard, in too much pain to even bawl. Bawlin's always a good sign. None of Barnes's men had a notion what to do. There was only that there young lass of his who seemed the least bothered. It was her, only a youngster she'd be at the time, who'd taken it into her head to come and fetch me.'

'A good girl, that.'

Hender shot Lannen a strange look, then went back to his tale. 'So I rolled my sleeves up and got on with it,' he said. "Course the first action was to push the calf back in and bring it round, so as to get the two front legs lined up with the head.'

'That's a mite easier said than done,' said
Lannen, watching Hender pause to grind his
spent cigarette into the floor.

'After that, it was a case of getting a lariat
round the legs and pulling until the head was out.
Me and the girl were still another two hours, I
reckon, easing out the body ... Barnes was
nowhere. Said he hadn't the stomach for it. Would
you credit that, Tom, it was all his damned fault –
and he hadn't the *stomach* for it!'

'What makes you say that?' Lannen questioned,
out of interest. 'Why d'you figure it was him who
was to blame?'

'Why, that calf was *big*.' He spread his arms
well wide. 'Must have been near the size of the
average six week old.' He shot Lannen a knowing
look. 'Only Barnes would have used a big bull on a
heifer like that, first time out. You see, he was
forcing the pace even then, trying to get out more
than nature intended. That's why he's overstocked now.'

'And you ain't?'

'Not me, boy,' said Hender, quickly. 'I can ride
this drought out. My land has been properly
farmed. The first signs I got my grass was
thinning and them pesky clams and tarweeds was
moving in, I eased off. Yessiree! But not Barnes.
He still kept on ... putting his bulls in amongst
them, like breeding was as easy as that....' He was
plunging two fingers of one hand in and out of the

loop of first finger and thumb of the other, in a crude gesture that evidently provided him with much amusement.

'This drought ain't gonna go on forever,' said Lannen, draining his glass and setting it down, in a way he very much hoped would bring this conversation to a close. He had a busy day ahead of him.

'I can't deny, though, Tom, I've taken a powerful fancy to this farm of yours. It's kinda strange, ain't it, I got so much land, more than a hundred and sixty acres of it, fully a square half mile of it, and you ain't got a quarter of that ... you got all the goddamn water!'

Of a sudden, Hender sprang up, giving Lannen a long, penetrating stare, the meaning of which he couldn't figure. Was it supposed to be an unspoken threat? He wondered.

'I'll be seeing you this afternoon, Tom. What time is it being held? Twelve o'clock?'

Lannen nodded and followed Hender to the door, watched him haul himself into the saddle then wheel his horse round. Then the big, blocky man had tipped his black stetson, jabbed with his spurs and departed with the speed and dust with which he'd arrived.

Lannen watched them until they had all but left his land. It was there, at the rise, that the troop of men reined in and Hender swung his mount round, as though as an afterthought.

Even without being able to clearly see his face,

Lannen could read his mind. Hender was thinking what it would be like to own Clearsprings Farm, Lannen's land.

SEVEN

Sheriff Dale Danvers brooded at his desk, the yellow wanted-posters that had just arrived, curling and crinkling in his calloused hands.

So, chances were the Tom Darling Gang was in the Territory. If they were, he *would* have trouble on his hands, trouble that would make this Lannen business look about as fearsome as a revival meeting.

He stared again at the names, matching them with the crudely drawn faces: Tom Darling, his younger brother, Jake, and fellow traveller, Con O'Brien. Each wanted in half a dozen states for bank robbery and murder.

He raised the glass with an unsteady hand, and cursed himself for ever having gotten into the job. What was one man up against those three, and the hoodlums who rode with them?

It was at times like this that he could have most used a damned good deputy. But he had no faith in Casey – whose youth and inexperience could have been forgiven if he'd been a trier. But Casey

couldn't have been described as keen and willing
to make shift at anything, even by his own
mother. He was a total waste of time. Good for
nothing but slicking his hair with fancy oil and
lounging on the boardwalk, smiling at every
petticoat that passed by.

What good was a jasper like that against a gang
famous for having shot three sheriffs – and scores
of others besides?

The more he thought about it, the more
dowie-hearted he became, and the more he'd have
liked to bring his fist smashing down into Casey's
face. He had a mind to if he caught him leering at
him like that again, as though he knew
something. But what could he know? How could
he?

He poured himself another slug and stared into
it, ruefully. He hadn't wanted Casey in the first
place; had never gone along with his appointment. He'd never liked him or trusted him. Even
at the beginning when he'd obviously been trying
to make an impression as a deputy, he hadn't
taken to him. There'd been his smirking
arrogance and something else, something about
him he just couldn't put his finger on. But it added
up to a heap of trouble.

But what could he, Dale Danvers, do about it?
Casey, who knew even less about keeping the law
than he did, owed his job to his uncle who was on
some goddamn committee somewhere. It was a
bad appointment but there was nothing now that

could be done about it. He took another long pull
and sat there, staring sullenly at the posters. No
doubt about it when Casey saw these he'd break
out into that grin of his. He'd be mighty pleased,
all right. He was just waiting it out till his boss
got a slug in the back ... that way he'd be made
sheriff.

Danvers lumbered to his feet, suddenly noting
the time was fast approaching noon. He drained
his glass, then made himself a determined fist, a
gesture of defiance against the world and of
contempt for his own weaknesses.

He'd be damned if he was going to oblige Casey.
Sure, he'd done his share of damned fool things in
the past, all kinds of shady, reckless deeds, but
from now on he was playing it cagey. He was
going to start acting mighty smart. He was
getting too old to take chances. Let these young
dudes, the Len Caseys of the world, take the
goddamned risks. He, Sheriff Dale Danvers, was
going to live a while longer, enjoy what this job
allowed him to put by.

As he walked out into the sunshine, life started
to become a whole lot sweeter. What had he to
worry about? Texas was a mighty big country.
And Plainsville? ... Well, the best thing that could
be said about it was that it was just about getting
on the map. Could be the Darling gang wouldn't
come within 500 miles of it.

And then a sly smile spread slowly across his
fleshy face. Whether the Darling gang came or

not, he would get something out of the rumour they were in the neighbourhood. It was common enough procedure when a gang was as notorious as Tom Darling's to blame them for every goddamned unsolved killing in the state. All he had to do was wire the federal marshal he was holding them responsible for the Lannen killing.

Of course, the telegraph clerk could be relied on to spread it all over town. That sure ought to get Tom Lannen off his back.

The sun was burning down from a brassy sky, the air hotter than the blast from a smithy, as the slow procession started. Soon the small wooden church was left in the distance and the incline to the burial ground, on the outskirts of town, began.

Lannen thought he was taking it pretty well until the arrival at the open grave. That was when his eyes started misting over but he kept his back ramrod stiff.

The coffin was being laid on the planks across the grave by black-garbed men, undertaker's men who doubled uneasily as sidesmen and shovellers at times like this. Preacher Cody, a wiry little man with the twitching face of a jack-rabbit, motioned a mite irritably for the party to gather round, Lannen just beside him at the head of the coffin, the other mourners on the other three sides.

With great ceremony the preacher opened his large black Bible and cleared his throat, just as he

had in the church, preparatory to reading in a
slow, sonorous voice, pausing frequently.

Lannen found himself watching the girl, Betty,
standing with her father. Her raven hair was a
perfect match for her dress which was entirely
black, making her clear skin the paler. Whether
her slightly built frame was supporting her father
or being supported by him, Lannen was not able
to judge. Certainly Barnes was puce in the face
and had seemed unsteady on his feet back in the
church. But clearly no one was finding it easy to
stand bare headed under a blazing sky. Perhaps
only Hender, who alone seemed at home in black,
had the air of a man totally unprepared to be in
any way moved by the circumstances. He just
continued to stare across the grave at Barnes in
implacable hatred.

The girl, to Lannen's mind, was mesmerized by
it all. He watched her gaze travelling in turn from
the hole in the ground to her father's face, then to
Hender's. Briefly she looked at him, and her
mouth worked trying to answer the sad smile he
was giving her. But it was too much for her and
she quickly looked away, down once more to the
grave. Finally, her eyes came to rest, vacantly, on
the sheriff.

Before Lannen had had time to take it all in the
undertaker and his helpers were easing the ropes
through their hands and slowly lowering the
coffin out of sight. Cody was sprinkling a handful
of earth and gesturing to Lannen to do the same,

while intoning, 'Ashes to ashes ... dust to dust....'
Lannen stooped and for a second held in the palm
of his hand the yellow earth, dry as dust. It was
not until he had thrown it down that the
gravediggers went to work, filling in, the noise of
their labour being drowned by 'The Lord's my
Shepherd.' Betty's voice wavered a little but made
itself heard amid the other deeper masculine
voices.

Then Preacher Cody was gripping Lannen's
hand, offering him deepest sympathies, and
turning to his horse. Within seconds he'd
departed.

High above, Lannen counted five big, black
circling birds, those heavy coyotes of the sky, that
in his opinion the Mex boys had the best word for:
zopilote.

Lannen was aware that there was a small group
of people standing around him wondering what it
was fitting they should do next. It was his place to
put them at their ease, he decided, and turned
towards the horses.

He found Betty at his elbow. 'Mr Lannen,' she
said, 'will you come back to the ranch now and
spend a little time with us? We could ... '

He was helping her into the saddle. As her left
leg went into the stirrup and the other one started
to cross over he could not help but see her ankles,
the lower calves looking smooth and shapely. He
looked away, angry with himself. It seemed like
an insult to Mary's memory and an act of

blasphemy at his son's funeral to be noticing such things.

Suddenly, behind him he heard the devil of a row going on. He spun round to witness a scene that would make a mockery of the girl's words.

Hender and Barnes were all but at blows with each other.

'What you accusing me of?' Hender was thundering.

'I'm accusing you of killing that there boy.' Barnes's thumb jerked in the grave's direction. 'Everybody knows you did it – and why you did it. You jest want Lannen's land.'

'If this wasn't a burying I'd make you eat your dirty words,' Hender was bawling even louder.

'Gentlemen,' the sheriff was saying, 'you cain't do this here and now. Uh, you gotta have some respect ... for the dead.'

Within seconds Lannen was across. 'This here is my son's funeral,' he said, the quiet firmness of his voice vastly outweighing the raucous loudness of others, 'and I ain't having it defiled by you two. Now, get the hell out of here, I want some time alone with my son.'

They went after that like two shamefaced schoolboys.

Betty was about to ride after her father, but checked her horse, momentarily.

'Er, Mr Lannen,' she said, unable to look at him, 'my daddy wouldn't have caused a scene like that for the world ... if he was himself. But these days he's, well, I can't explain it.'

'It's all right,' he said.

'He's very worried, Mr Lannen. Worried about everything. That's why he loses his temper so quickly.'

'Miss Betty, I know that. I don't judge him. He's got his worries. Who hasn't? I got a whole pile of them.'

'You're part of his,' she said, her hand for one brief moment darting out to rest on his shoulder. 'He's frightened Hender's gonna have you ... killed.'

EIGHT

Lannen was not a praying man, and his tongue felt as dry as a roll of tortillas wrapped in a corn husk but when, upon bended knees, he opened his mouth, he found the words pouring out.

'Oh Lord, give me strength to carry on. Give me the strength to see this thing through to the end … till I've found out who killed my boy. Then, Lord, forgive me because I surely will be taking upon myself the power of vengeance. Amen.'

As he walked back to his horse he noticed one person had stayed behind and was standing there, hat in hand, fanning himself.

'Uh, thanks for coming,' he said awkwardly.

'I wanted to,' replied Deputy Len Casey, smiling pleasantly. 'I knew your boy. He wasn't too much older than me. I used to see him every Monday riding into town. Most times we had a few friendly words whilst he was lookin' at the bulletin-board.'

Lannen was sure he could detect a change of attitude in the deputy from when last they spoke.

He seemed a whole lot easier today – but then yesterday he'd been delivering the worst kind of news.

'That there little rumpus, just now,' the young man carried on, 'it's all on account of this here drought.'

Lannen looked at the fresh, clear face, the smile tugging at the lips, the bright eyes, and wondered. If he was an acquaintance of Ben's, however casual, it was strange that the boy had never mentioned him. Because Lannen went so rarely to town, he'd always taken a powerful interest in everything Ben had to tell him about it, and for this reason the boy had generally spared few details of who he'd met, what they'd talked about.

Yet, not once, to Lannen's certain recollection, had the name of Len Casey cropped up.

'Thad Barnes and Zoot Hender ... those old boys is plumb up ag'in it for water. The way I hear it lot of their stock's bin frothing at the mouth and got the staggers on account of that old poison weed they bin feedin'.'

Without knowing quite why, Lannen was beginning to dislike this young man with the piping voice and confident eye.

'Look, I jest want to give you a piece of advice, Mr Lannen.'

Lannen was hauling himself into the saddle. He rested on the horn and, eventually found himself smiling, in spite of what he was feeling. 'I'm listening.'

'Don't take offence, Mr Lannen. I'm thinking of you.'

Lannen shrugged and bit his lip. There was no point giving utterance to his feelings, but he'd have laid a pretty large sum that whatever the boy was about to say had more to do with his own interests than any other man's.

'I think ... uh ... you'd do well to ... uh ... sell up and move some place else.'

'You do?'

The deputy appeared to frown at a thought. 'The way I figure it, your son weren't jest killed 'cos he were in the wrong place at the wrong time. That's what the sheriff thinks, but I don't go along with it.'

'So, what's your explanation, Deputy?'

Casey had swung himself into the saddle, so that he was on the same level. Though to Lannen's certain knowledge there was no one within half a mile of them, Casey turned round, in a rather exaggerated way, to survey the land-scape. When he spoke, it was in a low tone. 'I reckon it was a warning to you ... to get the hell out.'

Nothing had been more certain to Lannen from the beginning than that this was the case. 'And why would anybody want rid of me, Deputy?'

'It occurs to me, Mr Lannen, that they might want your water.'

For the life of him, Lannen couldn't be certain whether this was a guileless youth, voicing genuine concern – or a hard-bitten messenger of a final warning. 'Is that so?' he said. 'They might want my water?'

'Yeah, that's how I figure it.'

'Who might these folks be? Uh, these that want my water so bad they're prepared to gun down a young boy?'

The young man's eyes never flinched for one second; his round, pale, handsome face betrayed not the slightest emotion. 'Hell, I can't rightly answer that,' he said, after a thoughtful interval. 'If I could, I reckon I'd have to arrest them.'

'Is Danvers any nearer making an arrest?'

The boy was back to smiling again. It seemed, perhaps, he might enjoy any implied criticism of his boss. 'No, I can't say he is.' He favoured Lannen with a knowing pursing of the lips. 'But he's working on it.'

'What did those two drifters say, when he questioned them again?'

The blank face almost convinced Lannen there'd been no second interview. 'Uh, they described more clearly where they done found the body.'

'Has the sheriff been there?'

'Not to my knowledge.' Again that maddening smile. 'Matter of fact that's where I'm heading right now. I figure somebody ought to look at the scene of the crime!'

Was the boy looking for praise, Lannen wondered? Was that it, a young boy wanting an elder's approval?

'Wanna come?'

Lannen nodded his assent.

'That's what I figured you'd say,' said the deputy, with a grin. 'Let's git!'

Without further discussion, Casey jabbed his spurs in his horse's flanks and took off.

It was a strange pair who rode on together in silence, the older man in black, the younger one, a head in front, merely carrying a black armband.

It was the same drought-ridden country throughout their journey, almost unrecognizable from what it had been a couple of years before. Everywhere the eye looked it saw a vibrating heat rising and unlimited dust, dust that clung to the curling leaves of the drooping trees, and clogged the creeks. What had once been swollen streams were now dry gullies. Springs were pans of dried mud. Nothing moved apart from the two horses and the swirls of dust that pursued them.

The dry, hot breeze made Lannen wish he had a bandanna and under the savage glare of the sun he longed for his familiar broad-brimmed stetson and cooler clothing. It was the very blackness of his outfit that was attracting and absorbing the heat, where his usual dun-coloured clothes would have been slightly reflecting it.

It was while thinking these thoughts that his mind automatically turned to Hender. What kind of a Texas cattleman would be so plumb stupid as to choose to wear such clothes? It was about as crazy as one of them Eastern bankers marching to his desk in a pair of bullhide chaps.

Straightway it came to him – just as they were approaching Gerrard's Creek – that he might well be walking into a trap.

But then, if he wasn't safe with a deputy law-officer by his side who was he safe with, because even the most desperate of men would think twice before tangling with someone bearing the old five-pointed badge.

Then, unaccountably, Lannen's mind had strayed and he was back again to seeing those smooth calves and the foam of white lace he'd not been able to avert his eyes from....

The return to the Bar X Ranch was made in almost complete silence. Betty had not said a word since she'd caught up with her father, and he was just staring in front of him, lost in thought.

Eventually, with his own land in sight, he spoke in a cracked, tired voice. 'You think I was wrong back there, just now, confronting Hender?'

'Yes I do,' she said.

'It was ... wrong to do it in front of Lannen, I'll admit,' he said, grudgingly. Then he turned fully to face her, and there was something desperate in his eyes that frightened her but made her want to forgive him. 'But you know as well as I do that Hender's got that young boy's blood on his hands. I jest couldn't control myself, Betty. I had to speak my mind.'

'You'd have done a sight better saying your piece to the sheriff.'

'Pah ... the sheriff. Ever'body knows he's in Hender's pocket.'

Silence fell between them once more.

Back home, Betty walked straight into the weathered log ranchhouse and disappeared into her bedroom, intending not to reappear until it was time for her to fix the meal.

Funerals were always the most dreadful of occasions and they affected her very badly – but this one was the worst she'd known. The death of Ben Lannen was such a senseless waste. What possible reason could anybody have for a killing like that?

Desperately she longed for some peace and quiet but that was never to be found on a ranch. There was ever, day and night, the bawling of the cattle; but the hideous wailing of these starved and parched steers was something on a different scale. Even the hoarse shouts of the men working the herd seemed ten times louder than usual.

It came to her that Tom Lannen knew his business when he'd said that rawhiding was not for him. What it must be like out there on a drive, God only knew; it was almost beyond endurance back here on the ranch.

She went to the window, drawn by the very noise that she was trying to escape from. Outside, her father was pacing about, an unusual and unaccountably stupid thing to do under the sun's torrid blast.

She'd never known him like this before. He'd always been so sure of himself, so much in charge of his own destiny. To see him now, pacing in despair, was a sad sight. A sight as sad, in its own way, as looking at the brown waste his spread had become, or at a sky that promised no relief for those cattle that were bellowing relentlessly or, worse, lying apathetically on the dry ground.

Yet, she had faith in him. Somehow he'd come out on top. He always did.

In the meantime, maybe she could talk to Tom Lannen. If only he could just be persuaded to let their herd water once in a while. Surely that wasn't too much to ask of a neighbour? Lannen had more water than he needed. He couldn't help with the want of grazing but he could sure help out with that spring of his.

She realized she was coming round to her pa's way of thinking, and beginning to condemn Lannen as he did; equally, she knew it was the heart-rending sight of the cattle and, especially, the calves, that was making her. With an open mind, though, she could accept Lannen's frequently stated argument that her father's herd was many times larger than his own – and if he opened his spring to the Bar X it would very likely be sucked dry, and his own Herefords would perish.

So how would her daddy do it? How would he get the water he must get?

Suddenly, in spite of the heat, she found herself shuddering.

NINE

Since it was where his son died, Lannen travelled up Gerrard's Creek with a sick feeling in his gut.

It was a catamountain of a place at the best of times, a mile-long gully, spotted with yucca and mesquite, so different in character from the gently undulating range it cut through. It was the sort of place that won for Texas its reputation, among Yankees, of being either a whole heap of grass or a whole heap of desert.

Obviously it had been made by the stream, one of those that eventually found its way to the Red River, but in this drought was just a dried-up bed.

The two men dismounted and hunkered down, their eyes searching. Then once again they were on their feet and leading their mounts. Casey kept glancing high to his left as though trying to locate some landmark.

'You should have got them two drifters to show us the exact place,' Lannen said, testily.

The deputy did not reply, either because his thoughts were too centred on his task, or for some

71

other reason, Lannen could not be sure.

'Why didn't the sheriff git 'em out here?'

'Uh, them two drifters? I guess it's 'cos they can't be found.'

Lannen felt his anger rising. It was the first time he'd known intense rage since the second he'd learned of his son's death, and shortly after that it had subsided to intense sadness.

'You tellin' me them punks have left town?'

'I ain't tellin' yuh nuthin',' Casey drawled. He began to walk slowly, eyes fixed on the ground. 'But if yer askin', I'm sayin' I don't know where those punks are.' He spat. 'The sheriff don't exactly tell me these things.' He spat again. 'Matter of fact, I don't think he rightly knows himself.'

'Up there is where the shots came from,' Lannen said. He'd seen the scuffing of the brown earth where the horse had reared and the patch of dry blood, dark as red wine, and he'd no wish to see more at ground level.

Why the deputy had failed to read the obvious signs, he had no notion. Probably he was too dumb, or could be he'd gotten too close.

They tethered the horses to a cottonwood and drank lustily from their canteens before attempting the climb, right into the bright light coming over the crest.

At two flat-topped boulders, which would have provided ideal cover for the killers, Lannen stopped. He stared down gloomily at the track below. It was easy to picture the scene: the killers huddled here, watching the boy on the horse coming down the creek, drawing a bead on him, squeezing their triggers.... It would have been all over in seconds.

Then he went to work. He was down on his knees, his hand inching its way over the outcrop of rock. Though he was bending over, he could not but be aware of the deputy's complete lack of interest.

Finally Lannen's hand came to rest for a second and he threw the younger man a challenging look.

Its effect was that Casey broke into a grin and said, 'Mr Lannen, I gotta tell you you're wasting your time, there. If that's where they fired from, there'd sure as hell be shells lying here right on the rock.'

Lannen took out his knife and started to work at the place his hand had come to rest. It had touched something hard and flinty. 'Wrong, son,' he said, 'professional killers allus take their shells with them ... if they got time. It makes sense. Leastways, it would make sense to me if I'd just shot a party ... not to go leaving any goddamn shells that could be matched up with mine.'

He'd dug his knife into the hard ground a couple of inches, now. It was then that a fragment of metal came away in his hand.

He held it up. 'A broken spur,' he said, not without a trace of contempt in his voice for the boy who would not even have been looking here.

Casey took it from him and whistled. 'Waal, looks like one of the killers left behind his calling card.'

'Could be,' said Lannen.

'Whilst he was on his haunches, looking over the top, the tip of his spur jabbed in the ground and snapped off.'

'Could be,' Lannen said again, his eyes involuntarily straying to the deputy's own boots (as they would from now on to all men's boots), noting the pair of dirty but perfectly formed spurs.

Casey, catching his eye, grinned and continued slowly, 'Looks like this narrows it down plenty.'

'So what you gonna do now, Deputy?'

'Why, I aim to find me a man with a broken spur,' he said gravely. 'But it'll sure take time. There's two thousand men in Plainsville.'

'Yeah,' Lannen said, sardonically. 'Let's concentrate on just two of 'em right now.'

'If you're thinking of them two drifters, like I told you, I don't rightly know where they are.'

'Well, you'd better get lookin' then.'

Casey's face suddenly brightened. ''Course if we found them and one of them did have this piece missing....' He held up the fragment for closer scrutiny. 'It would only prove they'd been here. And we know that 'cos they found the body.'

'The body,' said Lannen, grimacing, 'was down there.'

'But they did say – it's in their statement – they took a look round, to see if the killers were hiding out.'

'Sure,' said Lannen, his tone even more sardonic. 'Sure. Those good old boys kinda risked their hides lookin' for killers hidin' out when it was no fight of theirs?'

Then to Lannen's surprise the deputy clapped him familiarly on the shoulder and said, 'Looks like you'd better come back to town with me, Tom. We'll take a look around and ... uh ... see what the sheriff thinks.'

Later Lannen would wonder about this.

TEN

Lannen really had no alternative but to spend the rest of the afternoon in Plainsville, even though work was piling up back at the farm. Deputy Casey had told him to call back at the office around five, by which time the lawman hoped to have located the two drifters – if they hadn't blown.

Lannen was particularly annoyed by the sheriff's absence, and it was that more than anything that made him agree to call back. He had things to say to Danvers that wouldn't wait for the morrow.

He had a light meal in Skelton's eating-house, his object not so much to take victuals, which he would have preferred to do at home, snatching a bite between chores, as to kill some time. Finding there was still a couple of hours to spare, he decided to do some digging of his own.

The Plainsville that he now found himself walking through had certainly kept on growing from its humble Main Street origins, that he remembered from his youth. In the last few years of Yankee development a parallel street had advanced, and three cross streets recently ensued. The brick-built Union and Western Bank and The Travelers, a two-storey frame hotel, were the town's oldest and most imposing buildings – but the rest, hastily constructed, were false-fronted establishments of various commercial enterprise, a good many being saloons.

It was these last that Lannen decided to check out.

It seemed logical to begin at the Lafayette, where he had last seen Kennedy and Townend, although he had little expectation of finding them there. The deputy could hardly describe them as having disappeared if they were still hanging round the saloon to which they had first been directed.

Predictably there was no sign of them and he left having done no more than eye the clientele. He did the same in most of the rest, one after another, merely walking through the batwings and staring at faces. In a couple he bought himself a bottle of beer, nursed it for a while, then left.

By contrast to those that he'd visited, Willie Mourne's, last on his list and at the far end of Main, was where the more respectable element drank, did business, enjoyed the crack.

Willie was a huge and genial man with the map of the Emerald Isle stamped on his ruddy face. Though he'd not seen his homeland for sixty years, his Irish brogue was just as strong now as the day he'd left.

'I'm surely sorry to hear about your boy,' he said. His eyes unusually were devoid of mirth. 'A lovely-looking boy he was.'

Lannen murmured his thanks.

'It's not a nice thing to hear a man's had to die. But it is especially not a nice thing to learn a boy's had to die. It offends against something in nature. What will you be taking?'

'I'll take a bottle of Lone Star,' said Lannen, 'and give me one of those long, thin cigars you keep.'

'I don't keep them anymore,' said Willie, regretfully. 'Hell, Tom, oul' son, that shows how long it is since you've been in Willie Mourne's. I've not been keeping them these three years. It's only the thick, fat ones I get asked for these days.'

'Yeah, it must be nigh on three years,' Lannen agreed. 'It's the farm, it takes twenty-four hours a day and more besides.'

Willie Mourne smiled at that, produced a fat cigar. He snipped it off at the end with a pair of specially tapered scissors, kept behind the bar for the purpose, and handed it over. 'Try this,' he said. 'I think you'll be liking it.'

Lannen nodded and dipped the chewing end in his beer. When he lit up he rolled the smoke round his mouth and let it ooze out slowly. 'It's mighty fine tobacco,' he said. 'I ought to get in here a darn sight more often.'

'That was the kind of boy I'd have liked for me own son, if I'd ever had one.'

'You never married, Willie?'

'That I never. And now I don't suppose I ever will.' He gave a hearty laugh at that, instantly suppressed when he remembered he was talking to a bereaved man. 'Sure, most of the women that I do meet in the course of business, you might say, are notorious. They're after me money. And me that's got none!'

Laughing loudly, Willie moved down his bar to attend to a sober-suited customer, returning a few minutes later. 'Tom,' he said, now adopting a low voice, hardly audible over the squeaking of the glass he was polishing, 'it'll be dem two drifters that's brought you into town?'

Lannen nodded. Equally quietly he said, 'Know where I can locate them?'

'You get to hear things in a business like this,' he said, giving a broad confident wink. 'They tell me they're playing cards upstairs at the Lafayette. They came with real big bucks and so far, bejasus, they've not been beat. They must have a whole mint of money now.'

Lannen's blue eyes sharpened. Maybe at last he was getting somewhere. Could be it was further proof that the two men were not drifters. Drifters and big bucks did not usually travel well together.

'Two from in here, Ben Kreuger and his pal, went to try their skill, yesterday,' Willie was saying, in the same quiet tone. 'Came back cleaned out. Said no one will beat that pair ... not with a pair of aces like ferrets up Carl Townend's sleeves!'

Willie was going again to the farthest part of his bar, and Lannen was going too, to the Lafayette. As he left, deep in thought, he was dimly aware of the Irish voice shouting, 'Don't leave it too long, Tommy-boy, before you come back again.'

Outside on the boardwalk it came to him that Willie Mourne was the only man in the whole world who had ever called him Tommy-boy. And yes he would come back ... come back and get himself juiced up. It had been a long time since he'd done that.

It had been a long time since he'd killed a man, as well.

Lannen sauntered into the Lafayette and this time ordered a beer. After delivering a few pleasantries, unreturned, he took his drink over to a corner table and sat down.

It was the stairs he was watching. But really there appeared nothing to be seen: No one went up or came down. If a game of poker was going on up there, there was nothing to suggest it.

There was no shortage of games of poker down in the saloon, however. Yet these were small time. That was obvious to Lannen at a glance. There were no big bucks on the tables and, more importantly, there was not the tension in the air that can always be felt when real gambling is taking place.

He ordered another beer.

As he climbed the stairs, watched by all eyes, it came to him that there was not much to choose in outward appearance between a man in the colours of mourning and the traditional gambler. There was nothing of fancy coat or vest on display upstairs, though, and the only black suit was his own, among the many men present.

The focus of attention was a large mahogany table where four men sat at cards; several others stood around watching events from a discreet distance. These last, to Lannen's eyes, were probably waiting to get on, taking the opportunity to observe what they could of other players' pokercraft.

Lannen sat down near the door. He was staring wide-eyed around the room, smiling to himself as he drank, trying to look for all the world like a grinning gaupus, the kind of sucker who might be cleaned out in one brisk game. Mostly, he was watching Carl Townend.

It did not take him long to identify all the men present. Not that he was on speaking terms with any of them but, Townend and Kennedy apart, they'd all been around Plainsville long enough, and been loud enough, to be known to most people, even the most retiring.

It was not the townsfolk he was interested in, though, it was the two new faces that fascinated him. His first glance had told him neither pair of shining boots was letting itself down with a broken spur. That was in the men's favour. So was the fact they were gamblers – in a way. He'd been right: they weren't drifters like they'd been pretending.

There could, of course, be an obvious explanation as to why gamblers should arrive in a town proclaiming themselves to be drifters. If they came advertising their profession, most folks would steer clear of their table.

He watched the smooth way they were operating, raising the stakes all the time. Townend changed two cards, filling them into his hand with deft movements, Kennedy, the banker, changed three and Jake Kettley, with a slight smile of satisfaction, only one. Len Driver, the fourth man, had evidently stacked.

In Lannen's experience, gamblers usually only have a mind to do what they do best, play cards, and do not moonlight as killers. If they did kill a man, it would generally be round the table, not out in a place like Gerrard's Creek. But he was wise enough to know that where gamblers were concerned there were no inflexible rules. A couple of gamblers on a losing streak might kill to bankroll themselves. It was like the ultimate gamble, since they were staking their own lives on not getting caught.

The game was ending in a stand-off between Townend and Kettley with the latter paying fifty dollars to see the other's hand.

Kettley had evidently missed his guess. Lannen

couldn't see the cards that Townend laid down, but they'd been enough to make Kettley throw down his own, stand up and push back his chair. He muttered something sardonic about his memory for cards obviously not being what it was – and left, taking Driver with him.

As Townend picked up the pot his eye went round to the standing men, a gesture which demanded to know who was next.

As the two townies, Clyde Hollinger and Russ Hammer, sat down, Lannen found himself on his feet and walking across. He'd been a good soldier in his day, good in every aspect of it, including the obligatory playing of a game called poker. In fact, he'd been damned good, one of the coolest in the regiment, but in those days he'd been playing for peanuts. And when seldom a day went by without a man would lose a good friend or comrade, he hadn't rightly cared too much about the outcome of a game of cards.

Whether he could still keep his nerve when the stakes were really high and his opponents professionals, he had yet to discover.

ELEVEN

Townend was already dealing and saying, 'Gentlemen, this is five-card draw poker, fifty cents ante, twenty-five cents if the pot is passed, minimum stake five dollars, no limits. Any objections?'

Lannen was hovering over Kennedy's right shoulder, a thing no man in his right mind would do. A woman might get away with it, find welcome even, especially if good luck seemed to coincide with her arrival. But a man, never.

Suddenly Kennedy spun round in his chair and swore savagely to the effect that Lannen should move off.

'Hey, is that game poker you boys is playin'?' Lannen drawled, unperturbed.

'I told you to **** off!' Kennedy shouted, spittle spraying from his moist lips.

Lannen calmly pulled up a chair and manoeuvred himself to the dealer's left, against the wall. 'Deal me a hand,' he said, grinning with as much semblance of idiocy as he could manage.

'They tell me there's big bucks to be won here. A friend of mine says plenty changed hands here last night. And I sure need to win me some.'

He fumbled in his shirt and from a money-belt took out the roll he always carried on him, having, like most smallholders, no great trust in banks. It was his working capital, money he could ill afford to lose – but what was money to him now? 'I sure feel lucky today!'

Kennedy was angry no more. He was back to smirking, as was Townend who said, 'You play much cards, fella?'

The speaker, like any good gambler, would never choose to go into a game without some knowledge of what he was up against, Lannen knew. So he'd tell him. 'Well, not since I left the army,' he said truthfully, 'but don't you boys worry none, I think I can still remember the rules.'

He was conscious that Townend, the red-haired, pig-faced one, though smiling broadly was mentally appraising him. The others, however, were barely able to contain their amusement. They were rolling their eyes and all but rubbing their hands together. This was going to be too easy, they were thinking.

It crossed his mind to open with the old bluff. He figured he might just get away with it, provided they took him for an easy mark. As he played it, he wondered if he should have known better than raise the opener, want no further cards and then put down heavily on the pat hand.

Surely they couldn't be that dumb!

They were scrutinizing him, wondering if *he* was that dumb. Had he got it or not, each probing pair of eyes was asking.

It was the smug smile, flicked on and off, that seemed the signal for them to fold. They evidently figured he'd just betrayed that he had got it.

'Well I'll be damned and double-damned,' said Lannen, raking in his winnings, 'I jest knew it was my lucky day.'

Round after round passed with Lannen playing the deadhead, taking small losses and getting out at the first opportunity, like he was only prepared to bet on a near certainty. Eventually he pulled his stunt with the pat hand a second time and won heavily with it. His opponents had taken some convincing but in the end had not been prepared to call to his twenty-dollar raise.

He fervently hoped the cocksure way in which he scooped his winnings, to say nothing of his general demeanour, would be enough to goad even professionals into behaving incautiously. This is it, he thought to himself, as he opened in the next game with another twenty dollar bet, no new cards required, smug smile on his face. It was only after laying down his money that he allowed his eyes to really focus on his hand, only to discover it was just about the worst he'd been dealt. He had a two of clubs, a four of hearts, a seven of spades, a nine of clubs and the ace of diamonds.

Kennedy's hawkish features had an oily sheen

of sweat as he studied his cards. He called for two, allowed himself a lopsided smile, then came on strong with a thirty raise. Townend immediately folded; Hollinger took three; Hammer, one.

After Lannen had raised another twenty, Kennedy shaking his head as though in disgust at this farmer's miserable bluff, said, 'I play these,' meaning he was also standing pat. Without a moment's hesitation, Kennedy raised fifty. Hollinger folded. Hammer whistled, straightened his stooping shoulders and raised a further fifty. He'd evidently got it into his head that both men were bluffing.

Lannen took another peek at his cards, then closed both hands round them carefully. He puckered his lips, thoughtfully. 'Raise a hundred,' he said, after what seemed an eternity, and alarmed by the crack in his own voice.

Hammer blew out irritably, peered at his cards as though for inspiration – and folded. His hand was, presumably, not strong enough for him to take the gamble, or he hadn't the nerve for it.

The stand-off was on.

Could be Kennedy was standing pat on a bust, or bluffing. It was Lannen's belief that he wasn't bluffing. There was a glint in his hard eyes that said he wasn't bluffing. Very likely Townend had slipped him the two ferrety aces. Certainly Kennedy couldn't have more than three aces. He took another peek at his hand, and smiled broadly.

'You cain't have a pat hand every time, feller,' Kennedy said, scoffingly.

'If you wanna know that bad, why ain't you callin'?' said Lannen, breaking his own poker rule allowing himself to be drawn into conversation.

Kennedy riffled his wad of greenbacks and then slowly lit a fat cigar. Even more slowly did he blow out the smoke in Lannen's face. Then, sensationally, he yelled, 'Raise five hundred!' and slapped down the amount in a way obviously intended to be intimidatory.

This was what Lannen had foreseen and dreaded. He would now have to ask for credit, as the bulk of his money was in the pot.

'I call,' he said.

'What with, sucker?'

'My credit's good in this town!'

'Like hell it is,' rasped Kennedy, his staring eyes even wilder than usual. 'If you ain't got the boodle to see my cards, you ain't seein' 'em. You're foldin'!'

'How much d'yer need, Tommy-boy?'

Never had Lannen been more relieved to hear an Irish accent. He turned to dart a quick glance at Willie Mourne standing next to him. 'I had a notion you might be needin' some funds,' he said, genially, bringing down a big hand on Lannen's shoulder. Would you be wantin' just the five hundred – or, maybe, a little more.'

From out of his back pocket he produced just about the fattest wad that Lannen had ever seen.

'Now you sure you'll not be wantin' to raise, Tommy?'

Lannen smiled. 'I've already called,' he said regretfully.

'That don't matter,' was Willie's weighty opinion. 'You haven't put down, boy. Dat means you can still raise.'

'Suits me,' said Kennedy, gruffly.

'In dat case, he raises a thousand,' said Willie, peeling off a large slice and tossing it down.

Kennedy's bulging eyes were transfixed by the pot, then he smiled that leering, crooked smile of his and said, 'Hey, Carl, gimme a thou!'

With some reluctance, as Lannen judged, Townend took out a billfold from his inside pocket and laid the sum on the green baize, in a neat pile which contrasted with the disorderly heap.

'And here's two hundred more I'm raising,' said Kennedy.

Lannen batted back his hat and rubbed his brow. There was more money resting on the table than he had ever seen in his life. His hand had now found its way to rubbing his chin. It seemed that Willie Mourne might have more money than these two. Should he try to drive them out. Was that his best chance? 'I call,' he said, at last.

Kennedy slowly and with considerable flourish flicked over three aces, one after another, and then his hand with just as much swagger began its dash to the pot.

TWELVE

'You raised on three aces?' said Lannen, grinning mischievously. 'I got me four kings!'

Kennedy's hand stopped in mid-flight. There was a raw, deadly tension rippling the air. Then the sudden silence was no more as Willie Mourne started to dance an Irish jig.

'Like hell you have,' Kennedy boomed, his face puckering horribly and a nerve at the side of his eye starting to tweak.

'Like hell I *have*.' He turned them over as slowly and theatrically as had his opponent.

The dumbstruck loser was staring at Townend, who was shaking his head.

For a long moment Lannen sat there gawping at his winnings, as though he, himself, was unable to take everything in. Then with all eyes on him he let out a bellowing whoop, of the sort that would not have been out of place at the end of a 500-mile cattle drive and said, 'Well, hell, I'll be doggone … if I ain't just bushwhacked a travellin' gamblin' man….' He put his head back and laughed out loud. 'Well, I reckon I'll take my winnings home, now.'

'Like hell you will!' thundered Townend, even louder than his partner had recently shouted.

Lannen frowned like he was expecting trouble and was unused to it – but still he went on calmly picking up the pot with his left hand, eventually holding up the big catch and letting it flex in his fingers like a freshly tickled big green trout.

'Like hell I *will*,' he said, repeating his verbal trick of some moments earlier. Suddenly his lean features had become taut, and his blue eyes stared chillingly at the seated company. His face was unmistakably that of a man as far removed from the fool they had taken him for as it was possible to be.

Kennedy swallowed hard, found his gaze drawn to the slim, wiry fingers of Lannen's right hand, which somewhere in the discussion had unobtrusively found its way to rest on his hip bone – no more than two inches away from the smooth handle of his Peacemaker.

If none had seen it make its discreet progress there, could be they'd been concentrating too hard on his greedy left paw.

'Two men came to this town yesterday,' he snapped, 'bearing the body of my son. I reckon I've just taken off them the money they was paid to kill him.'

He stared from one to the other of them and a silence, unearthly considering the number of

people present, hung over the whole room.
Lannen smiled thinly. 'I don't intend to take any
more money off you boys, that's if you've got any
more to take!' He started to ram the bills in his
left-hand pocket. 'If you cain't beat me with
Townend capping the deck with that pair of aces
he keeps up his dirty sleeve – then double-dealing
them to you – well, I guess you ain't never gonna
beat me.'

Lannen's eyes again challenged each of them,
passing quickly over the two townies who both
looked like they wished they were any place but
Texas, coming to rest on Kennedy.

He was desperately hoping to get him riled up
enough to give something away. Townend, he was
pretty certain, would never give anything away.
Though their faces had remained as impassive as
only poker players could when he'd mentioned
Ben, they'd both started to boil at the exposure of
their sharping.

It was only the capital crime he was interested
in. He would have to try something else.

Kennedy's wild eyes started to bulge, disbelievingly, when registering that Lannen's gunhand had moved away from its poised position
and had come to rest innocuously on the table.
The change in the gambler was instantaneous.
'Boys,' he said, in a tone even more menacing than
anything he'd used before, 'I think this here dumb
nester is callin' us cheats!'

'Hell no. I wouldn't say that,' Lannen drawled.

'You boys have just lost big. Mighty big! Some cheatin' that, eh!'

'Well in that case, mebbe we're saying you're the one that's been sharping.' It was Townend's turn to speak, no doubt as a diversion.

Kennedy's hand had whipped out his gun, but Lannen's boot was faster, coming up with a stunning ferocity, sending the weapon whirling in the air.

Instantly Lannen's back had arched and he had sprung to his feet, his own Colt riding high. With the same trusty boot he sent Kennedy's gun skittering across the floor to Willie Mourne who picked it up with a grunt and trained it on the seated card players.

Nursing his right fist in his left armpit, Kennedy squirmed in his chair. 'You're gonna pay for this, Lannen! We want our money back, and sure as hell we're gonna get it back!'

Lannen shrugged and started to back out, wondering what, if anything, he'd really accomplished. 'You've lost money!' he bellowed angrily. 'What I've lost I can never get back. If you want to clap your filthy hands on this here bankroll' – he jerked a thumb at his pocket – 'you jest come tell me who paid you to kill my son. And make it soon.'

The moment they were out on the street, blinking in the bright glare of the sun, Willie Mourne clapped him on the back and said, 'Hell, oul' son, you've really put the cat among the pigeons now.'

'That's about what I intended.'

'And where, if I might be askin', did you learn that little trick wid de four kings dat went south when, sure, nobody was lookin'?'

'In the army ... you saw me?'

'No, that I did not!' Willie sounded quite indignant. 'I saw you put your hands together to bring 'em out, like you was prayin' to the Good Lord ... and I knew what you were after.' He turned and gave a conspiratorial wink. 'In my day I was the best hand mucker in all of Ireland!'

'I palmed 'em one by one during the earlier rounds,' Lannen laughed, bringing out of his sleeve four more cards, 'then I switched them from there when I needed 'em.'

'When they find they're playing with a deck that's lacking, they'll be coming for you Tommy-boy!'

Lannen shrugged. 'Let 'em come. I've sure got a bigger score to settle with them!'

'When this gets out about how you play cards,' Willie chuckled, 'it'll mean the end of your reputation for honesty in this town, you know.'

Lannen shrugged again. 'Being honest has always kept me poor,' he said, taking out his winnings with a certain pardonable pride and starting to count out what he owed. 'Thanks for stakin' me, Willie. You were running a helluva risk with your money, you know.'

'Not at all. Not at all.' The grey eyes twinkled. 'Not for one minute did it ever occur to me that you might lose.' He tapped his nose. 'A good judge of character is oul' Willie Mourne.'

They shook hands. 'Thanks, anyway,' Lannen mumbled.

'Don't mention it. Take care Tommy-boy.'

With that the oldster skipped off down the street, leaving Lannen with his thoughts. Yes, he had achieved something: now they'd have to come to him. And when they did, they might just bring their boss with them.

THIRTEEN

'He ain't back yet,' said Deputy Len Casey, grinning, arms outstretched in a gesture supposed to mean *Hell, I've no idea where he is; he ain't the kinda fella mighty partickler about time!* 'Sit down, Mr Lannen, have a shot of whisky.'

Lannen joined Casey at the desk and, as he sat down, found a bottle of McQuaid's and a glass being slid in front of him. It was, in fact, precisely the sight of the specially imported whisky that determined him to leave.

'Thanks Deputy,' he said, 'but I guess I've cut the trail dust from my windpipe enough for one afternoon. I gotta get back to the farm.'

'He said to wait.' Casey had sprung up also, and was wiping his grin away with the back of his hand, along with a dribble of the expensive liquor. 'He can't be long now.'

'I've got me a cow that can't wait, either,' Lannen replied, determinedly, 'and ten thousand other chores to do. If Danvers has got any information for me, let him send a message.'

'This sure is mighty good whisky you're turning up,' persisted Casey. 'And *uncommonly* rare in these parts.'

'I know,' said Lannen, allowing himself a tight smile, 'I've got a bottle of it at home.'

Casey raised his eyes, disbelievingly.

'Given to me by the same generous person who made a present of it to your boss, I'd wager. And your boss, by the by, might get *uncommonly* sore if he finds we've disposed of it for him.'

'Mr Lannen, it's my duty to advise you not to go back today.'

'Not go back?' What in tarnation was the boy saying? 'I gotta go back. I've got a farm to run.'

'You're mighty welcome to one of our bunks for the night.' Even though he was obviously trying desperately hard to be all formal and official, a grin escaped him as he added, 'We've sure got plenty of them.'

Lannen was anything but amused; he widened his eyes incredulously. 'Sleepin' in one of them would seem to me to be too much like being in jail!'

'Mr Lannen ... it's my belief you're in powerful danger, if you don't heed my warning.' He writhed in his chair. 'I cain't do nuthin' to protect you if you step out of this office now!'

'*You* can't do nuthin' to protect me!' Lannen thundered. 'Listen, sonnee, I'm mighty beholden to you for being so concerned over my welfare but I don't need your goddamned protection. I can take care of myself.'

'I believe whoever killed Ben is gonna try to git you.'

'Yeah,' he agreed, nodding his head, exaggeratedly, 'I sure hope so. I'm kinda counting on it. 'Cos that represents just about my best chance of finding out who the hell it is out there that hates me that bad.'

'With a bullet in your brain, you ain't gonna be any wiser, mister.'

If he allowed the boy the last word, it was simply because he hadn't time to stand around jawing. Home was where he was going all right, but not to drink McQuaid's. He mounted up and spurred away unusually quickly, forbearing further conversation with the deputy who'd come to the hitching-rail, an anxious expression clouding his youthful features.

It had come to Lannen with a terrifying certainty that someone had wanted him in town all afternoon. The deputy had only been doing someone else's bidding.

And that could only mean one thing.

Had Lannen not been so intent on speed he might have listened to the warning bell clanging in his head. He might have thought twice before riding blind through Gerrard's Creek. But even if he'd turned it over a score of times he'd still have gone on because the only other way back would have involved a wide detour, through other folks' land, and cost him a good half-hour.

Nevertheless, he had the sense to slow his horse to a canter just as he approached the narrowing of the trail, the spot where his son had been so mercilessly gunned down.

His horse snorted its unease, its ears pricking up. An eerie silence surrounded him. Long, grey shadows were merging into the heat-haze, making everything indistinct along the ridgeline of the gully. He found himself staring steadily and expectantly at the two boulders where earlier in the day his eyes had been dazzled.

Suddenly the silence was torn apart by the slam of a rifle shot, the echo cracking and winding the length of the gully. He actually saw the flame of the muzzle, a split-second before his left shoulder received a terrible blow. Though glancing, it was of such ferocity that it all but knocked him from his horse. The brown, squealing in terror, reared and lunged sideways, which might have saved Lannen because twice more the air cracked.

His own weapon was out and, as he dug his knees into the animal's flanks to steady it, he was emptying all six chambers in the direction of the boulders. Then he was spurring away round the bend, jumping from his horse and smacking her on the rump, all in one blur of action. The horse bolted, as he intended it, but he knew she wouldn't go far, being of too docile a disposition to stray, even after coming under fire.

Hunkering down behind a rock to get his breath back, he delved into his sidepocket for shells.

Taking the Peacemaker between his knees, he began to feed the chambers. Only then did he check his left arm which was throbbing like hell. He could move it, which meant the shoulder wasn't bust, but it was mighty painful.

Next, he found himself worming his way up the slope, pushing through brush and mesquite. The pain in his limp arm was now intense but, strangely, it seemed to trouble him not at all, so great was his desire to get up and confront, at whatever personal cost, his son's killer. There would never be a better opportunity than the present.

About halfway, he stopped to take stock. His ears were straining to pick up a sound but there was nothing save that of his own shallow breathing.

He was aware, too, of the blood trickling down his arm, and the crazy thought came to him that he'd ruined his best suit.

When the sound came it surprised him. It was the beat of hooves, rapid and quickly thinning to a distant thud. Could be it was a decoy, one man leaving, while one or more stayed. The rifle shots had been spread out, though, suggesting they came from one rifle – and he figured his assailant for one man, working alone. He realized, as he stood up, that if he was wrong in his surmise, he would pay a heavy price for it.

He braced himself for the worst but nothing disturbed the quiet and, with the light fading fast, he made his way, as quickly as possible through the scrub, to the bald summit. It was behind the two large rocks that he found the shellcases, three of them, .44 calibre and probably spat from a Winchester. This time the gunman had not had time to carry away the evidence.

But a moment's thought told him the gunman would have had ample time to pick up the shellcases, if he'd a mind to. So had he just panicked and ridden off? That would not have been a very clever thing to do. Why surrender the advantage of the high ground? The moment he descended from the ridge, he had risked a bullet in his own back.

Then it came to Lannen that maybe this assailant was not of the party that shot his son. They used handguns, probably Colts, which meant they'd been pretty confident of their ability. If they weren't they'd have used a rifle.

On the other hand, if one of the original gang of killers had just now, for whatever reason, decided to go it alone, he might well have decided to play safe and use a rifle, especially as this time he was up against a man, not a defenceless boy.

All this was conjecture. What was certain, however, and the most puzzling of all, was that a rifle had failed to find the true target, where Colts had succeeded.

It was almost full dark when he approached his own farm. He'd been riding slow, on account of the pain in his arm.

He breathed a sigh of relief even to see Clearsprings in black outline. It was all there, roof and all. It had crossed his mind that it might just be a charred shell. Folks wanted his land – and his water – and burning a man out was not unknown. It seldom failed, in fact. Very few farmers who'd experienced it had the appetite to start over again. Especially with the likelihood of a second burning.

A wise man, of course, would not venture far from his own door while all this was going on. At least that way he'd be there to protect his property if it came under attack. But then, he mused, such a man would not be in a position to find out who killed his son – or, more importantly, kill whoever killed his son.

Then another wave of fear came over him. Why was the milker not howling in pain? She'd been left longer even than yesterday when she'd bawled enough to raise the dead. All afternoon long she'd been on his mind. Normally nothing would induce him to leave her this long, or to put any dumb animal through that kind of pain. But the death of a son kind of cut across the usual domestic concerns.

He tied his horse to the rail and walked slowly and philosophically to the barn. He had a strong feeling he was somehow surrendering himself to fate. But what else could he do? It was quite likely that those who wanted him dead were waiting somewhere around the farm in ambush. That, of course, would explain why the polecat back there in the creek had given up so easy.

The only thing he could do was draw his gun, which he did, and hope for the best.

As he entered the barn he was as near as dammit certain of some presence there. He felt a tightening in his gut and a sweat start to break out. He stood there motionless for several seconds, his narrowed eyes trying to cut through the dark. And then came the shifting of a stall's timber and he knew what it was ... and started to feel somehow as foolish as relieved. It was the unmistakable sound, a second later, of a contented cow chewing the cud, that made him laugh out loud.

Striking a lucifer, he stared around him. The milker was there all right. And so next to her, amazingly, was a pail with a muslin cloth over it. He picked it up, felt its weight, heard its slosh. Milk. He breathed in its sweet, fresh smell. It was still warm.

Then he was swinging round, roused by the scraping of the barn door. Blinking at the figure holding a kerosene lamp in one hand and a nickel-plated six-shooter in the other, he said awkwardly, 'So ... uh ... you're the milkmaid!'

FOURTEEN

'Mr Lannen,' she gasped, her hand flying to her mouth, 'your shoulder! You're hurt. What happened?'

'I stopped a slug,' he said quickly. 'What you doin' here, Miss Betty? And what's this gun all about?'

'I brought it with me,' she said, giving him a long stare and moving closer. 'I kinda thought you might be in trouble.'

It was her expression, which most strongly held his attention. He could not read its meaning and say whether this beautiful girl was sad or lonely or frightened – or even if she was wistfully reaching for something beyond her.

She was at his elbow now, her fingers tenderly pressing the muscle just below his shoulder. 'Let me bandage that for you,' she said. 'We gotta boil up some water and get it cleaned, then you'll have to get to the doc's.'

He let her lead the way, like it was her home not his, and sat there patiently while she went about lighting the stove.

He winced as she took off his jacket and then ever so slowly eased away his shirt. She carried them both over to a chair and he was surprised to see her going through his pockets, as though it was a perfectly natural thing to do. She evidently found what she was looking for, the bag of makings in his shirt pocket. Strangely, she completely ignored the thick stack of bank notes.

Then she was expertly rolling a firm, slender stogie, twisting the ends of tobacco back into the pouch. She put it to her lips, lit it and inhaled. Finally she placed it between his lips. 'I learned to do that for my pa,' she said, 'when he bust up *his* shoulder.'

He watched her glide over to the dresser, following the lines of her dark green blouse and riding skirt which fell from a slim waist the full length to her ankles. He found himself smiling at her embarrassment, given away by the unsteady hand that poured out a large measure of her pa's whisky.

'You got some bandages?' she asked, as she gave him the drink.

He was standing up to get them when she gently pushed him down.

'They're in that cupboard,' he said, pointing to it. 'But, Miss Betty, it's getting late. You shouldn't be here. You still ain't told me why you are here.'

'This bit won't hurt,' she said. She was standing over him about to clean the wound.

It was a long time since a woman had been so close to him. He'd forgotten what it was to be touched by a soft and feminine hand.

'Liar!' he said, grimacing.

'Wait there. Don't move.'

'I ain't about to.'

She was back in seconds with a wad of lint. He watched the expression on her face, trying to judge from it how bad was the wound she was probing.

She smiled as though judging his thoughts and said, 'It's pretty deep, but I'm certain there's no bullet there. You'll still have to see a doctor, though.'

'I can't leave here,' he said. 'I've got to be here. I can't afford to leave this place unprotected.'

'Mr Lannen,' she replied, in a faltering voice, 'that's what I've come about.' She was winding the bandage gently but firmly round his shoulder, under his arm and over. 'I've come to apologize.'

'Apologize!' he repeated. 'For what?'

'My daddy ... er ... brought his whole herd on your land today. And watered them good and long.'

The sigh he breathed was one of relief. He ought to have guessed it. If that was all his delay had been contrived for, and nothing else had happened, well he could live with that. 'I don't rightly blame him. I guess I might have done the same.'

'I begged him not to,' she said. 'I begged him to just ask you. I said you were a good man – you'd have let him, wouldn't you?'

The imploring face before him, unreally pale in

the lamp's dancing shadows, was loveliness itself. Dearly would he have liked to be able to say something, anything, that was kind. 'No,' he said, slowly, 'I wouldna. I'd have said no.'

She drew back from him. 'But why, you've enough water? My pappy's always been a good neighbour.'

'Waal, mebbe I'd have been wrong. But I've got a duty to my own herd. And jest lately that there spring's been getting thinner and thinner. If this infernal drought goes on, I don't believe I'll have water much longer.'

'But you've got it now,' she said, almost inaudibly, 'and our cattle are dying.'

'And so are Hender's and a lot more. If I give water to one, I'd have to give it to all. And I can't do that.' He smiled as best he could. 'I'm real sorry.'

'I know that, Tom,' she said, softly, then added, 'I've got to finish this bandage now, so hold still.'

It was the first time she'd ever called him that and it sent a shiver clean through him.

'Thanks for doing the milking,' he said. 'I shouldn't have left her so long. I'm blamed if I know why I did. I just kinda got held up.'

'You couldn't help it ... if someone took a pot at you,' she said, sympathetically.

'No, I'm talking about earlier in the day. I shouldn't have gone back into town with Casey. I don't know why I did.'

She was back near to him now, winding the

remainder of the bandage into place. Her gentle breath was on his forehead.

'I'm doin' everything I can, see, to find out who killed Ben. It may take me a sight longer than an experienced lawman, of course, 'cos I've never undertaken a job like it before, but....'

It was when she bent to put her teeth to the bandage that her breast lightly brushed his chest. She was trying to make a tear in it so there'd be two strips to form a knot. It was a tough bandage and she was having difficulty.

'But I'm goin' to ... uh ... have a darned good try,' he added.

'I reckon if any man can do it, you will, Major.'

'Why d'you call me that?'

'You were a major weren't you?' she said, picking at the end of the bandage. 'You got some scissors?'

'Er, no,' he said.

'You weren't in the army?' she sounded disappointed. 'Daddy said you were a major. And a very brave one!'

'Oh that,' he laughed. 'Yeah, I was in the army. I meant I don't have no scissors. Is a knife any good?'

'It doesn't matter,' she said lightly, 'I'll manage. Anything for a war hero!'

'I was in the Confederate Army,' he said, 'fighting against those folks from up north where you and your pappy come from.'

'I know that.' She gave the bandage another

bite. But, heck, that don't stop us from admiring your courage, that folks round here still talk about. They do say single-handed you charged a field-gun to stop it firing on your men.'

Then for one delicious moment her breast settled itself against him as she made a greater effort to bite into the material.

Involuntarily, his own arm had gone up and placed itself round her waist.

She carried on tying the bandage for a second, and then settled into his arm. He would wonder afterwards how he had dared to touch her – and figure he wouldn't have, if he'd had time to think about it.

She smelt so goddamn nice. And felt like an angel.

A long time later she raised her head from the pillow to look at him and said, drowsily, 'Tom Lannen, you're a hell of a man, did anybody ever tell you?'

'What's your pappy going to say about you stayin' out all night?'

She laughed, a light tinkling, happy laugh. 'You're gettin' carried away, mister. I ain't stayin' out all night. I'm goin' now. Well, soon.'

'He'll be mighty sore with you, if I know anything about Thad Barnes.'

Something was evidently amusing her. 'He will be *mighty* sore – if he finds out. But he ain't about to.'

She was pulling on her blouse and skirt now, putting out of sight all that lovely white flesh he'd not been able to tear his eyes away from.

'I wasn't dumb enough to tell him I was going out.'

He watched, mesmerized, as she took a blue ribbon from her mouth where she'd been holding it, and started to wind it round the crocheted top of the white stocking he'd just run up her leg. Deftly, she did it up in a bow then doubled the top of the stocking over it.

'The very idea of his daughter going out apologizing to you....' She made a clucking sound through her teeth. 'And if he knew the lengths I'd had to go to ... to make it right with you....' She laughed again. 'Well, he just wouldn't have allowed it.'

Having run up the other stocking, she was looking round with consternation on her face.

'You sure he didn't see you leave.'

'I came on foot,' she said, snatching the blue ribbon from him, which, coyly, he was holding out in front of him.

'You left it in the bed,' he said.

'And I'm sure he didn't see me go callithumpin' out my bedroom window.'

She'd turned away this time to tie the knot, as if his eyes had seen enough for one night. 'If he'd seen me, he'd sure have come after me.'

She was combing her hair, which tumbled to her shoulders in a rich, dark mass, glistening and lustrous in the lamplight, using a comb of his she'd picked up from the dresser. This pleased him.

'I'll walk you home.'

'You will not. And with that bad arm of yours!' Then her eyes widened and she snuggled against him. 'Although I'm pleased to say your injury has not totally incapacitated you.'

He grinned. 'Least let me go with you to the end of my land.'

'Yeah,' she agreed, 'it's your land. You can do what you want on it.'

'Yes,' he said, reflectively, 'a man should be able to do as he pleases on his own land.'

Suddenly, more than ever he was determined he was going to keep it. His land.

FIFTEEN

Lannen had a deal of farming matters to catch up on. Though a small farm it was almost impossible to run it with just one hand. And he was literally down to that, the stabbing pain in his shoulder making it quite impossible for him to move his left arm.

Nonetheless, he was up at first light, making shift to get things done, putting more hay in the horses' manger, pegging out clothes on the sagging line, turning the cow out to grass, collecting the eggs and scattering meal. Hardest of all was to get on horseback and steer his herd to the water-hole, not that they needed much encouragement. As usual they broke into a shambling, bellowing run when they smelt water.

As all morning long the sun climbed the long slant of the eastern sky, he laboured on, determined to get everything done that had to be done, so he could have the afternoon free. But around noon he felt himself wilting in the intense heat and realized it was more than just heat. His strength had ebbed away unusually quickly as a man's does when he has been wounded.

He set himself down on the porch and was taking a slug of whisky to dull the pain and to give himself the burst of energy that alcohol brings for his final chores, when he saw the lone rider on the far hill. Big and bulky, whoever it was had reined in his horse and was reconnoitring the area.

The rider seemed satisfied with what he'd seen and was coming in now, slow, and carefully quartering the slope rather than taking the direct route.

It was Thad Barnes, Lannen was now sure. Normally this was a man in a hurry, but evidently not so today.

'Cracked shoe,' he cried by way of explanation, as he reined in, then added, 'what's happened to you, soldier?'

Lannen found his gaze straying to Barnes's saddle, but there was no Winchester in the pouch, no rifle at all, in fact. And there were no spurs on his silly half-boots.

'Some critter took a shot at me last night.'

'Hender?'

Lannen shrugged. 'Might have been you, Thad, for all I know!'

This at least checked the man's smile. 'Tom, don't joke like that. Listen, I kinda owe you....'

'I figured it was you made free with my water.' He had to protect Betty. 'You or Hender.'

'It was me,' he said, smiling again, 'and being a

man of honour, I'm going to pay for what I took.'

'Seems to me a man of honour would have asked first before he took what rightly didn't belong to him.'

'My steers were dying,' he pointed out. 'Tom, I had to do it. And, hell, it made no difference to the level of your water.'

Lannen wondered if that was what Barnes had been trying to estimate, from his position high on the hill, before venturing in.

'So you're figuring on doing it again?'

'I'm willing to pay. Next time I come I'll pay you mighty well for what don't cost you a goddamn cent.'

Lannen felt like reminding Barnes that he had yet to take out his billfold for yesterday's ration. 'The way I feel at the moment, I'm more likely to swear out a complaint to the sheriff that you've been on my land with your herd ... illegally, than to accept *any* offer.'

'Sheriff Dale Danvers?' Barnes laughed, helping himself to a long swig of McQuaid's and sitting down heavily on the porch. 'They tell me he's all tied up right now chasing the Darling Gang!'

'How much?'

Barnes studied him. 'Not exactly in money, Tom. Times is hard. Capital I ain't got right now.'

''Spect you've spent it fetching in all these mighty fancy things.' He held up the bottle to make a point, but Barnes seemed to interpret the gesture as an offer. He took the bottle and started to guzzle breathlessly.

'Tom, I can give you better than money.'

'What might that be?'

'Protection.'

'Protection?'

The big man placed a hand on Lannen's arm and shot him a knowing look. 'I thought that might get you interested.'

'Protection ... from what?'

He felt himself being stared at again, and the look on Barnes's face was one of pure disbelief.

'Why, from Hender, of course. He's trying to run you out. Hell, if he can't do that, he's gonna kill you. Like he killed ... uh ... Ben.'

This really got Lannen wild. One-armed or not, he found himself grabbing Barnes and pulling him to his feet. 'When you mention my son,' he rasped, drawing his gun and jabbing it into the fat belly, 'and try to make personal gain out of his death, you better be sure of your facts.'

Barnes was wheezing hard and the purple veins were standing out on his contorted face. 'I'm sure, Tom. I'm sure. I wouldn't accuse no man – not even my worst enemy, like Hender – if I wasn't damned sure.'

'Give me one reason why I should believe you.'

'That's what I've come to tell you,' he said, leaning against the rail to steady himself.

Lannen took a step back. 'I'm listening.'

'Hender's in town at this moment. He's been talking to the two men who did it. Killed Ben.'

Lannen holstered his gun. 'Where did you come by this information?'

'One of my hands was in town this morning … saw Hender by himself go into Willie Mourne's. He figured that was peculiar. Hender never goes anywhere without his bodyguards and he's not the kind who frequents bars. So he followed him in, saw him talking to two dudes. Money changing hands.'

'So what does that prove.'

'The two dudes were Blake Kennedy and Carl Townend.'

Lannen wasn't saying anything; he was listening and thinking. He was puzzled why two such as that should choose Willie Mourne's, of all places, to collect, knowing the owner of the place a friend of his. Was it their way of answering his question: who was their paymaster? Why would they do that?

'So you tell me why Hender should be paying those two!'

'OK Thad,' he said at last, 'if this is true, it looks bad for Hender.'

'It's true, Tom, on my honour.'

Lannen knew all about Thad Barnes's honour.

Hender left Willie Mourne's deep in thought. He'd just parted with $2000 and wanted a return for his money. But could he trust those two? Would they deliver? If they were true to their word his problems should soon be over.

What were a couple of thousand dollars when so much was at stake? His hope was that they would get on with their undertaking with all due speed.

Even as Hender was riding in one direction, Kennedy and Townend were walking in another, determined to win back their losses at the card table before they did anything else.

'This business has to be handled with care,' Townend said, the derisive laughter deep in his eyes.

'Yeah, I guess Mr Hender's gonna have to learn patience,' Kennedy remarked, equally amused.

'There's no need to rush things.'

'Hender's good for at least one more payout.'

'In fact,' said Townend, taking out one of Willie Mourne's cigars and stopping to light it, 'all we gotta do is sit tight for a while.'

'Yeah, play some more poker. Now that Lannen's beaten us, there'll be plenty of others wanting to try.'

Townend's face had twisted brutally, all trace of humour gone from him. 'Hell, we risked our necks to finance us and then like a couple of tinhorns we let that farmer take it off us at our own game.'

'We shouldn't have let him just walk away with it like that,' Kennedy growled.

'If there'd been a shooting, maybe the sheriff would have had second thoughts about believing our story 'bout what we seen in Gerrard's Creek!'

Just as suddenly, as they turned into the

Lafayette, they were both back to snorting with laughter.

'The darnedest thing is,' said Kennedy, 'that two thousand bucks Lannen took off us ... it kinda belonged to him in the first place!'

SIXTEEN

There was a persistent throbbing in his wounded shoulder, a throbbing which grew more demanding and agonizing the more he rode. He twisted in the saddle to try to ease the pain but if anything it made it worse.

It was difficult to believe that this was only the third day. The first had been the death of his son; the second, the burial; and this, the third, what would it provide? Three days, three journeys into Plainsville, each one eventful in its own way. He had no doubt this visit would be.

His first stop was the sheriff's office. He'd no wish to step outside the law, unless of course the law proved itself about as rotten as one of those pustulating boils on Danvers' face. His message was to be simple: Kennedy and Townend had been seen in Willie Mourne's receiving a second pay-off for their dirty deed. What was he going to do about it? He would not mention Hender at this stage, not because he had any reason to doubt what Thad had told him but simply that he had no

121

wish to complicate things. And as Thad said, Danvers was in Hender's pocket. But, then, with Thad supplying his whisky, could be the lawman was in more pockets than one.

Let's keep it simple, he said to himself. Let's go one step at a time, and see if Danvers is serious or not about bringing in the hellions who killed Ben.

In the event, he did not deliver any kind of message because once again Danvers was not in his office.

'He ain't never here these days,' said the grinning Casey, who was at work on yet another bottle with a red and yellow label. It had to be a new one because it was only a couple of slugs light.

'Know where I can find him?'

'Not exactly. He got a whisper that the Darling Gang was holin' up 'bout fifteen miles outa town ... and he's gone to check it out.'

'What, by himself?'

'Nope, he took a posse with him.' He grabbed another shot. 'I said I'd go along but he kinda declined the offer.'

Lannen looked the boy up and down and was not entirely surprised.

"Course the sheriff thinks kinda highly of those two gamblers, if that's what you wanna see him about,' Casey went on, looking closely into Lannen's face. 'He don't believe they're killers, like I believe you do.'

'And what might you believe?'

'I believe ... they sure might be. Hell, somebody must have killed your son.'

'When did Danvers leave?'

Casey opened the drawer of the sheriff's desk and took out a crumpled sheet of yellow paper. ''Bout nine o'clock,' he replied, stretching out the wanted poster in Lannen's direction.

'Who gave him the tip?'

'You're askin' too many questions, Mr Lannen. That's lawman's business.'

'Who gave him the tip?' He took out his roll, now swollen considerably, and started to reel off bills. He stopped after laying ten dollars on the desk, and put the rest away.

'Seems to me you're tryin' to bribe a U S deputy, and that's a mighty serious offence in this state.'

'Why, I'm not fixing to bribe anybody,' Lannen said, 'I'm just counting out ten dollars ... for your welfare fund.'

'In that case, why don't you count out ten more?'

'And then you might jest remember where the sheriff came by his information?'

'I might and there again I might not!'

Lannen scooped up the money. 'Now that I think about it,' he said, 'I ain't that mighty interested.'

If life had taught him one thing, it was never to haggle with jaspers like this. Make the offer then walk away if it's refused. Most times you got called back for the acceptance.

Casey was on his feet. 'OK, ten dollars and I'll

tell you. Hell, there ain't no big secret 'bout it, anyway.'

Lannen put the greenbacks back down on the desk and then to Casey's surprise sat on them. 'I'm listenin'!'

'It were ... Zoot Hender. He came in real early, said late last night one of his hands had spotted a whole group of horses outside the old Marriot place, other side of Shand Ridge. It's been disused for years.'

'Somehow squatting in a disused farmhouse don't seem to me to be the Darling Gang's style.'

The deputy shrugged. 'Mr Hender sure had a powerful notion it was them. He even lent out his men for the posse.'

'I take it Zoot Hender didn't go along for the ride as well?'

The smug way he was leering suggested Casey maybe knew something else that Lannen didn't. 'Nope, Hender had other business to take care of in town, I believe.'

'Enjoy your whisky,' said Lannen, as he left.

It was not until he'd got halfway along Main, chewing things over, that the sudden thought overtook him. It was as he flexed his arm that it registered: Casey had not even mentioned it. His wound.

That was a mighty strange thing ... unless. Unless what? Unless he knew about it already!

Lannen's second stop was Willie Mourne's – just

to have it confirmed that Hender had been there and in the company of Kennedy and Townend.

'That's the strange thing about it,' Willie said. 'After yesterday's malarky, I wouldn't expect them to be socializing in Willie Mourne's. And, sure, the man in black's not been in above twice in thirty years, and dat's no word of a lie!'

Willie had even spotted Cy Lacey, one of Thad Barnes's men, come in a little after Hender had arrived. It was all exactly as Barnes had described.

He rode back real slow, weighed down with thought. It had to be Hender. Whichever way he looked at it, it kept coming out the same. Most damning of all, Willie had seen a heap of money being handed over.

So what had Hender been paying – if not a second instalment on Ben's murder? Kennedy and Townend had been cleaned out, and, naturally enough, had gone back for more. But why, as seemed likely, had Hender deliberately manoeuvred the sheriff out of the way? Suddenly, it came to him as clear as day. It had to be his own death that had just been transacted, and either Danvers was being got out of the way to make it easier – or he was in the know and just wanted an excuse to be well clear.

He figured they'd all kind of take it for granted he'd be holed up at home. Maybe Kennedy and Townend had already been there, gunning for him. In which case, finding him absent, could be they were back in Gerrard's Creek, hoping to accomplish what last night in the fading light Hender failed to do.

Things were at last beginning to hang together. It had to have been Hender last night. The lone rifle. It had to be. He'd gone back there himself hoping to do the job. Having screwed up, he had no choice but to hire out the same assassins.

It all fitted.

Yet, somewhere at the back of his mind, there was still the nagging doubt that had been there from the moment Thad had told his story. It all seemed so pat – like one of the pat hands he'd bluffed with. Too damned pat!

Whatever else Hender might be, he was certainly not a fool. Surely if he was going to take out a contract on a man's life, the last place he'd be seen making the pay-off would be Willie Mourne's with a weight of solid citizenry there to witness it, not to mention the owner himself, a known friend of the intended victim. Unless, of course, desperation had made Hender completely reckless. Perhaps even an intelligent man becomes a hopeless fool when he's desperate.

He did not in the event go through Gerrard's Creek. It cost him half an hour or more in time, but he met no one as he traversed other farms and had an uneventful journey.

One thing that none of the critters would expect was for him to be heading where he was now heading.

* * *

Had Lannen taken his usual route, in all probability he would have encountered Betty Barnes, galloping at full tilt to town, looking for him. Having called by Clearsprings and found him gone, she'd naturally assumed town was where he'd be.

She had an urgent message for him.

SEVENTEEN

When the lawman arrived he found Barnes in the yard, immersing himself in physical work in a vain attempt to take his mind off things. Unusually in denim pants and check shirt, both heavily sweat-stained, he was toiling away, hammering in a fresh stake for the section of fencing he was repairing.

When Barnes saw his visitor he stopped, fanned himself with his brown stetson and grinned. 'C'mon in,' he said, 'and let's have a shot of your favourite Scotch. I've sure worked me up a powerful thirst.'

He led the way in and from a cupboard took out the McQuaid's. It was the last bottle and he stared at it, wistfully. He regretted now having given so much of the stuff away.

'Whisky's just like water in one respect.' His voice sounded thicker than usual and all of his visible body was sheened in sweat. 'You sure never miss it, until it runs dry.'

He poured two good shots and passed one across

to his visitor. The light seemed to glance off the five-pointed star on the man's chest and for one second to wink in the glass he was holding up before him.

'Your health and prosperity, Mr Barnes,' the man said. 'Now that Lannen's done found out about Hender, could be things will work out purty fine for you.'

Barnes drained his glass and automatically refilled it. 'Could be my two neighbours will kill each other,' he mused. 'Then I might just get me a heap more land.'

'And plenty water for your whisky!'

Barnes laughed at that.

The two men clinked glasses.

Lannen topped a rise and took a track that clung to the ridge, and headed in the direction of the big spread he was visiting. At last he reined in and dismounted.

It had been the same in the old days: always before going into battle he would equip himself as best he could, paying attention to every detail that might conceivably save his life or his men's. He checked and rechecked his weapons, adjusting the sling he'd rigged up for his left arm to make himself a bit more mobile, then sat down on a rock to stare thoughtfully at his boots.

He allowed himself a few moments' ease and, as he smoked, the memories came flooding back to him. Most of all he remembered Ben's early years, when life seemed to hold out so much. The war was over and having survived it how could a big, strong, hard-working man like him fail, with a wife like Mary by his side and the boy to help him, especially with land like he'd acquired, the Promised Land that he'd set his heart on since he was a boy.

Forever green and lush it was, and he was going to rear cattle on it and fatten them on its green slopes. With a spring like that it would never know drought. Farmed well, as he fully intended to farm it, it would yield all that his heart desired. And one day it would be Ben's for him to hand down to his son, Lannen's land.

He stood stiffly and flicked away the butt of his stogie, a bitter gesture.

Finally he stashed his money, scooping away the iron-hard earth from under the bear-shaped rock he had sat on and which he could never fail to know again.

He had taken out all the insurances he could.

He approached the ranch-house with a beating heart. He'd come to kill a man and expected to either succeed or die in the process.

As he looked about him at the bare, dry inhospitable land it was easy to see why its owner had been so desperate to take over Clearsprings. Brown earth stretched as far as the eye could see, patched with green cactus brush. Slowly his gaze turned to the ranch buildings. It was a good place, he thought, with nothing fancy about it. The house itself was built of adobe and wattled boughs, flanked by corrals and outbuildings. Out back was a neat horse-paddock.

He stopped before entering the gate and listened. What caused him the greatest concern was the extreme stillness of the place. There was no sign of human-beings, only the distant muted bawling of the herd.

He rode up unchallenged to the hitching rail, dismounted and tied up next to the lone black horse. He adjusted the gun on his hip, then straightened to his full height and started to walk towards the door.

Suddenly that same door was flung back and Hender appeared. There was a smile on his ruddy countenance and he was extending a hand. 'Tom, come in,' he shouted. 'This is a real nice surprise!'

Lannen walked in, grim-faced. The apparent warmth of the welcome had kind of thrown him. It was like he was dropping by real neighbourly.

'Tom, is there something troubling you?' Hender sat himself down in one of the large chairs and gestured his visitor to do the same.

'You bet there's something troubling me!' Lannen rapped, declining the offer.

'Well ... uh ... get it over with, then! Say whatever you've come to say, boy!'

'I've come to kill you!'

The old man visibly blanched. 'To kill me....'

'Yeah, like you killed my son ... you or somebody in your pay!'

The rancher attempted to get to his feet but slumped back down again, as Lannen drew.

'So it was you who arranged for my men to be got out of the way? You started that fool story about the Darling Gang being holed up. Either that or Danvers is in cahoots with you.

'Zoot, don't insult my intelligence. I ain't plumb stupid. I know the message about the Darling boys came from you. I guess you sent your own men with the sheriff to make the story more believable – or to make sure he stayed out there.'

'Tom, you've just lost your son; it's been a powerful shock to you. It's disturbed your mind....'

Lannen continued to train his gun steadily on Hender's chest, but he was finding it mighty hard to pull the trigger.

'Tom, let's talk this out. You gotta give me a break. If you figure I killed Ben, you gotta tell me why.'

Why he should be listening to this, even considering explaining, Lannen didn't know. He'd come to do a job. He'd best get it over with. 'Let me see your boots,' he snapped.

'What?'

'Your boots. Turn round so's I can see the spurs.'

'Now I know you've gone plumb loco.'

'Just do it!'

Hender climbed wearily to his feet and turned round slowly. 'Satisfied?' he said, as he resumed his seat.

Lannen would have been more satisfied if

there'd been a broken spur. 'OK,' he said, 'so you're clean on that one. Now, I want you to take your gun out ... real easy. With your left hand. And I want you to thumb out the bullets one by one.'

Here at last would be the final proof he needed. Hender, the man in black: black hat, black coat, black tie, black pants, black boots, black horse ... black heart.

'It's the black bullets that's gonna tell me you murdered my son.'

Hender was shaking his head, vigorously, a look of desperation on his craggy features. 'No, Tom. No....'

It was then that Hender, seizing the moment Lannen was gawping at the first bullet to bounce on the ground, brought the Colt arching upwards, the finger of his left hand circling the trigger and crushing hard. There was an ear-splitting explosion, a puff of smoke and a spurt of flame that went lancing past the target's right shoulder, splintering the wall behind.

Lannen's own gun spat fire. Hender jerked under its brutal slam, then struggled to his feet, hanging there unsteadily, eyes writhing, his whole vast frame twitching like a puppet on a string. He was staring at nothing with a look of immense astonishment. His hands were clutching his chest, and he was slowly crumpling to the ground.

'Tom....' It was a hoarse, gurgling whisper. Then

his hand, now flat out in front of him, slowly formed itself into a fist. 'You've got it wrong, boy....'

Lannen bent over him and turned him on his back. He was stone dead.

He shut the staring, sightless eyes and then tried to straighten out the bunched fingers that had closed round the bullet, the last action of the dying man. They would not be prised away, as if rigor mortis was instantaneous. It was only with vast difficulty that he managed to open that claw enough to bang out its contents.

The bullet was just as Lannen had thought he'd seen it. Instantly he retrieved the dead man's gun and rolled the chamber, flipping out the remaining bullets, one, two, three, four.

They were all standard issue. Nickel.

He would have wished it otherwise. Had they been black, he would have felt better about having shot the man.

But the fact Hender had ordinary bullets proved nothing, he told himself, as he straightened up. Could be it was one of his accomplices who had the black ones. Then a stronger idea came to him. If a man had made a killing and in doing so had left his trademark behind him, chances are he'd sure change his slugs. If he had any sense, he would.

He'd had his revenge on the man who'd ordered Ben's death. Revenge was supposed to be sweet, but there was nothing but a heavy weariness about him now as he crossed to the door, desperate for air. It was not the weariness of a man knowing there were still two more deaths ahead, Kennedy's and Townend's, it was the weariness of a man who felt he'd done all the killing he should ever have had to do, back there years ago on that bloody battlefield of hot hell at Cold Harbour.

It was as he stepped on to the porch that he heard the click of a trigger being cocked and the guttural snarl, 'Hold it right there, Lannen!'

EIGHTEEN

He turned round real slow and with a sickening lurch in his gut saw the warped grins on the faces of Kennedy and Townend. He ought to have reckoned on them being somewhere round their boss.

'Well if it ain't the great poker player himself!' said Townend. 'Mighty clever trick you pulled mucking those four kings in your hand.'

'Yeah. You want me to show you how it's done?'

'I want you dead, mister,' Townend returned.

'And I'm gonna be the one who kills him,' said his partner, hugely amused.

'We'll work upwards,' said Townend. 'And see how many shots it takes to finish him.'

'I shoot first,' said Kennedy, a fierce light in the staring eyes.

'You kill me now,' said Lannen quickly, 'and you'll never see your two thousand dollars again.'

Townend's gun had already bent so that it was training on Lannen's kneecap. 'What two thousand dollars might that be, boy?'

'What I took off you at poker!'

'We're gonna be well paid for killing you,' said Kennedy.

'You ain't gonna get another cent. Your paymaster's dead. I jest shot him.'

The two jaspers looked at each other in exaggerated amazement. 'You just killed Hender, right?' said Townend.

Lannen nodded.

Townend scrubbed a hand across his stubbled jaw and angled his fiery head to one side, as though to tell the world he was a deep thinker. 'Well, this sure makes it a whole lot easier for us. Now we can say we killed you on account of you murdering our good friend, Mr Hender.'

A smirk passed between the two of them.

'I got the money back at my farm stashed away,' said Lannen. 'I can get it for you.'

'That's mighty nice of you, friend,' said Townend, 'and when we've shot you into ribbons, we might jest mosey over there and take a looksee, ourselves.'

'You boys done pretty well out of this.'

'Pretty well, indeed,' said Kennedy, a gloating expression on his face.

'What with the money you got for killing my son. And what you've just been paid for killing me.'

'Yeah. You're 'bout right there, boy,' said Townend.

'You ain't about to deny it, then, that you killed my son?'

Townend snapped his mouth closed as though he might be, then he shrugged. 'No,' he said indifferently, 'why should we?'

Kennedy was still grinning mirthlessly. 'It gives us satisfaction to let you know, before we kill you.'

'You're just scum,' said Lannen, capturing Townend's casual tone.

The man's eyes narrowed beneath the flame-coloured eyebrows. 'I'm gonna take personal delight in shooting you,' he snarled. 'You pulled a gun on us in that there card game. And we don't like having a gun pulled on us. It makes us mad, see! And we don't like no claypole like you taking our money off us at our own game.' He cocked his trigger. 'This is one I'm gonna enjoy!'

'Get on with it,' said Lannen, tersely. 'Don't stand around jawin' – if you're gonna shoot ... shoot!'

He braced himself for the inevitable. It seemed like an eternity was passing before him. Everything had slowed down and the surroundings become highly magnified. The gun he was looking down was a cannon held by a giant.

'I reckon the money will be in his shirt,' said Kennedy, 'jest like it was yesterday.'

'Yeah right,' agreed Townend. 'He wouldn't leave it no place for someone else to find ... nesters ain't like that.'

'No, he ain't that dumb.'

'He's dumb,' sniggered Townend, 'but not that dumb. Search him!' Then he laughed loud, putting

his head back and exposing the badness of his
teeth. 'Hell, we don't want our money all full of
holes, now, and a mess of blood.'

Kennedy advanced towards Lannen and jabbed
his Colt in his gut. 'Get it off!'

Oblivious to the pain, Lannen eased the sling
away, then started to unbutton the front of his
shirt. He was about to shrug himself out of it
when Kennedy ripped it from his back.

'I ain't got no poke on me. I told you, it's back at
the farm.'

'Take your boots off cowboy,' said Kennedy. 'You
look to me like the kind of ornery old chawbacon
who might jest keep something squat down there.'

Townend grinned at that. 'That ain't a bad idea,
Blake. That sure ain't. It wouldn't surprise me
none.'

Kennedy aimed a vicious kick at Lannen just
below the knee. He was glad to use it as an
opportunity to keel over.

'Get them boots off, boy!'

Slowly, Lannen pulled off his left boot and
threw it across to Kennedy.

Townend had drawn in closer. He was smiling,
wryly. 'When a man takes off his boots seems to
me he takes off the right one first,' he said. 'If he's
right-handed like you is!'

'The other one,' Kennedy demanded, his eyes
widening with anticipation, and closing in for it.

Lannen bent forward again and even more
slowly this time, began to tug.

Then with an amazing speed that later he would marvel at, he was rolling over. Derringer in hand, he was firing off at Kennedy, praying his one shot found its target, watching the gun spinning from the man's hand, watching the blood come spurting from his heart, his legs starting to buckle.

Townend gave a bellow of rage and started to fire, the bullets snarling out and thudding heavily into stomach lining, laying bare the knotted guts.

It was the human shield that saved Lannen, as the big carcass of Kennedy fell backwards on to him and would have covered him had he not twisted clear, his hand closing on metal as he jack-knifed up amidst a resounding crash and a swirl of smoke.

The bullet that homed into Townend with a force that sent him sprawling, and left him bleeding in the dust, was from Kennedy's gun. Lannen realized this some moments later as he attempted to holster it. Providentially, it had dropped where he had been able to reach it.

'Yeah,' he said, more to himself, really, 'I sure did have me something down my right boot, you dumb bastards! Thank God for that.'

The silence that followed was eerie.

Townend had been lying stock still as though dead but all at once he began breathing out low sobs like a mortally wounded animal. If he'd been a horse, Lannen would have put him out of his misery. As it was, he merely searched him, as he had his partner. But they had not a single black bullet between them. Townend's billfold was bulging with crisp ten-dollar bills bound together, as well as a wad more of dirty notes.

'This,' said Lannen, extracting the newly minted, 'is what you were paid to kill me. I don't reckon on you needing it no more.'

He pocketed the pelf. Together with what he had already stashed he'd quite a deal put by for … a dry day!

He dusted himself down, restored the torn shirt to his back, the sling to his shoulder, and then picked up his own Colt. It was the weapon that had saved his life, the lady's purse gun, the much derided Derringer, that gave him pause. As he weighed it in his palm, he was marvelling at its potency. For all its lightness, it was as effective as any gun in the world at close range and with a shot to the heart.

It was a trick he'd learned years back in a bar in Laredo, when an ageing huckster had pulled one out of his shoe. And the look on the dying man's face came back to him now. One of sheer surprise mingled with rage that such a peashooter should have done for him. Kennedy's staring eyes were still registering just that emotion.

The victor was mounting up. Instinct was telling him to get the hell out – pronto. With their boss dead and two more bodies on hand, Hender's men were not going to ask too many questions.

They were going to shoot first, think later.

He was on the point of spurring away, when unexpectedly, he heard his name being grunted, loudly and urgently. He turned quickly in the saddle, wondering if there was more life left in the pig-nosed one than he had supposed. The gaping hole in his chest said not.

He was once more about to give his horse the nudge.

'Lannen … you killed … the wrong man....'

The words sent a chill right through him. He almost jabbed in his spurs and bolted his horse, not wanting to hear more but he could not close his mind to it.

'Lannen, d'yer hear me? You got the wrong guy.'

He dismounted and approached the prone figure. He did not fear it was a trick. It did not cross his mind the man might have a hidden weapon hidden about his person, in the same way as he had done. He knelt over the red head, trustingly, guilelessly. Somehow he knew those handful of gasps he'd just heard were speaking true; in his heart he knew it.

'Lannen, it was a set-up!'

So saying, Carl Townend died.

NINETEEN

'Well, I best be getting back to the office,' he laughed. 'I bin away an awful long time. People is gonna start missin' me!'

Thad Barnes stood up and extended his hand to the speaker who, strangely, remained steadfastly astride his seat. 'But not Lannen,' he said. 'He's off your back now.'

'That was one smart move, Mr Barnes. If Lannen's done killed Hender, I shall kind of enjoy arresting him.'

Barnes smiled engagingly and sank down again. 'Don't be too damned quick about doin' your duty in that line,' he said. 'We gotta give those two gen'lemen a fair crack of the whip. If they earn their money and kill Lannen, it'll save the town a hanging.'

He laughed at his own humour and refilled his glass though not that of his visitor. 'I never did like a hanging,' he went on, 'it brings out the worst in men. How the whole town can stand there gawpin' while some poor devil's twitching his last, I don't know.'

The sudden thud somewhere in back had both of them on their feet. Then Barnes twinkled amiably. 'That'll be Betty,' he said. 'She thinks I don't know she climbs in and out of her bedroom window. The Lord knows where she gets to.'

He lumbered to the door and threw it open. 'Betty, that you?'

There was a long moment's silence before, 'Er, yes, Daddy,' came the cry. 'D'you want anything?'

'Uh no, darling. I'll see you soon. I've just got a little business to finish up.'

'Well I guess I'll be going then,' said the lawman, putting down his glass but taking no steps.

Then Barnes smiled with understanding. 'How stupid of me,' he said. 'I ain't paid you, yet.'

The lawman grinned. 'Well, yeah, Mr Barnes ... we made a bargain and I kept my part of it all the way down the line.'

'It's up to me to honour my side of it, eh?'

'That's about it, Mr Barnes.'

The big cattleman sighed and ran his finger down the side of his nose. 'Let me tell you summ'n. There ain't no honour involved when you make a deal with a man about murder.'

'Hell I ain't done no murder, Mr Barnes.' The speaker's eyes narrowed but he managed to force a laugh.

'No you ain't. And that's to your eternal credit. But if the truth ever came out, you'd hang like the rest of us 'cos you're just about as involved as any man could be without actually pulling the trigger. And you an officer of the law and all!'

'So you ain't gonna pay me … is that what you're figurin'?'

'Hell, did I say that?' said Barnes, throwing out an arm in an avuncular gesture. 'Sure I'm gonna pay you but you're gonna have to wait some. I ain't got it at this moment, but I will as soon as I get me Lannen's water. I can raise plenty of capital on that.'

'How long's that?'

'A day or two. A week at the most.'

The lawman put his hat on at last. 'OK, no problem; I can wait.' He laughed, unnaturally. 'You had me worried for a minute there, Mr Barnes. Hell, for one moment I really thought….'

'What did you think, boy?'

'Well I thought you was about to go back on the deal.'

A pleased smile crossed Barnes's dull features, giving them briefly a liveliness they did not often possess. 'Think,' he said, tapping his head. 'Why would I do a thing like that? I need you as much as you need me. Folks put a lot of faith in a feller if he's carryin' that old tinstar. When I've got me Lannen's water, not to mention Hender's land, why Thad Barnes is gonna have this town in the palm of his hand. I'll need the sheriff on my side.'

For a second a frown came on the lawman's face, before understanding dawned and he broke into a wide grin. 'I'd sure appreciate it,' he said, 'if you was to help me to become sheriff.'

'I owe it to you,' Barnes said, a note of sincerity in his voice. 'You've done well … I'm beholden to you for the way you got me them two killers. And another thing I won't forget: I saw the way you took care of Danvers and talked Hender into making our boys that offer to expose me, when all the time he was setting himself up to take the rap. That was good. Mighty good!'

The two men were breaking out into fits of near hysterical laughter. 'Mighty good indeed!' Casey wheezed.

Suddenly their features froze. Barnes's eyes were dead, like a cod's. 'Mighty good indeed!' had come back at them like an echo.

With a swift, explosive movement Lannen entered the room, his Colt pointing midway between them. 'Seems like I've heard it all now,' he said, sardonically.

'Not everything,' came another voice, a woman's this time.

'We met on the road,' said Lannen, standing to one side to allow Betty in the room.

Shock possessed her. Even on such familiar territory, she had a lost look. 'I gotta know, Daddy, I gotta know why you did it?'

Barnes surveyed his bonny, black-haired daughter, his eyes coming to rest on the nickel-plated gun in her hand. 'You've helped this man into my house,' he thundered, jerking his head in Lannen's direction, 'and you now pull a gun on me. My own daughter!'

'My own father, a common murderer!' Her eyes were holding level but her voice faltered. 'Why? Why? Why?'

'No,' he said, 'not that. I ain't that. Call me anything but that!' He shook his head. The whisky tumbler looked small and fragile between his hands. 'I never killed him. It were Kennedy and Townend, they shot him. They was only supposed to put the frighteners on the boy, to make Lannen more persuadable. Hell, they sure weren't supposed to kill him. That weren't part of the deal.'

'Daddy I wish I could ... I....'

'On your mother's soul, God help me,' he said, lifting an imploring face to her, 'I knew nothing about the murder. It was those two – Kennedy and Townend – gettin' carried away. You gotta believe me, Betty. I wasn't even there.'

She'd taken a step towards her father. 'Daddy, I do believe you,' she said. 'I gotta believe you.' Then she turned to Lannen with a look beseeching such trust from him. 'I gotta believe him, Tom. 'Cos if he's lying it makes him the worst kind of evil under the sun.'

She swung back to the man being discussed. 'I can't believe you'd accuse Hender over that boy's grave ... if you'd killed him yourself.' A look of horror pinched her face. 'You couldn't do that. No one could!'

'Believe me I had no part in the killing, Betty.'

'Bull,' said Lannen, quietly and matter-of-factly.

'It's true, I tell you, every word of it. Ain't that right, Casey?'

The deputy was nodding his head in vigorous assent.

'You gotta believe me, Bet.'

'He did it,' said Lannen, 'and those boots of his prove it.'

Barnes looked down at his working boots, registering incomprehension.

'One of the killers left half his spur behind ... and unless my eyes are deceiving me, you're half a spur short!'

'Didn't I tell you to git that fixed?' Casey snarled.

'Shut up!' Barnes yelled. 'Keep your mouth shut, Casey!'

'And I don't doubt if we take the bullets out of that six-shooter of yours, they'll be the colour of the grave where you're going.'

'No, Tom.' Betty's voice was desperate. 'No, Tom. I can't believe he did it. Not actually shot....'

Lannen wasn't going to make the same mistake with Barnes he'd made with Hender. 'Take his gun off him, Betty, and see for yourself. There were two black bullets in Ben's heart, fired at point-blank range. Check his gun.'

She appeared to be about to go into a swoon. Her face had slumped down and she'd relaxed the gun in her hand so it was pointing at the floor. Her free hand went to bury itself in her raven hair.

'I don't need to,' she said, in a quiet scream, 'I don't need to. I know he shipped in a case of black bullets a while back ... same as he ships in everything.'

'Even professional killers,' Lannen added.

It was at that moment Barnes went for it. Lannen knew he was going to, maybe even before he knew himself. It was in his eyes, his slow, bulging, drink-sodden eyes.

'No!' he heard her scream, feeling her weight slam against him as his Colt spat out. He would wonder after if the injunction had been to her father or to him – or to both of them.

He had been aiming for her father's gunhand. The fact that he hit him in the brain was because the girl jolted his arm. She was staring dumbstruck at where his head had been.

In trying to save his life she'd killed him.

Lannen had already decided that never would he tell her this.

Casey's hands were already held high, an unbidden gesture. 'Mr Lannen,' he jabbered, 'you keep me out of this. You say I was only here to arrest him and I'll back your story up all the way.'

'Kill him!' Betty screamed, furiously. 'Kill him! But for him my daddy would be alive now. He's been hanging round here for months now. I used to think it might be me he came to see. But no, he was only here to try to inveigle himself into my daddy's pay.'

'Don't you listen to her, Lannen, she's crazy.'

'I know how much plotting and scheming he came to do because my pappy used to send me out when they was 'talking business'.' She turned to stare at Lannen. 'I heard 'em last night talking about you, Tom. I heard your name mentioned. That's why I came lookin' for you this morning to warn you. Casey was about to have you killed. I know it!'

'That's not true, Miss Betty. I only ever did what Mr Barnes asked. It was he that approached me to find him some killers. Why, he even took a shot at Lannen last night, and I didn't know a thing about it 'till I saw the sling on his arm and I guessed what had happened. It was your father who planned everything. Everything!'

'Liar!' she screamed, as she brought up her pistol and squeezed its trigger. 'Liar!' She continued to pump lead into him. 'Liar! Liar! Liar!'

Her face ashen, she did not look vengeful any more, only sick and hurt.

'You didn't oughta have done that,' Lannen said, gently taking the weapon from her trembling hands and getting her out of the room. 'You ought to have let me take care of it.'

'You wouldn't have shot him.'

He sighed. 'It gets easier when you've shot one.' Turning her face to his, pointedly he said, 'Casey went for his gun, remember?'

He wasn't sure whether she understood because she just collapsed into his arms. For long minutes he thought she was having some kind of screaming convulsive fit. After a while, though, like a storm it blew itself out and she was just a sobbing little girl. That was when he carried her into her bedroom and left to get the sheriff.

EPILOGUE

Under a sultry sky, oddly hazed grey-green, the colour of desert cactus, Sheriff Dale Danvers and Tom Lannen rode slow. Before leaving, they'd both had liberal measures of whisky, finishing the remains of the Old Crow (which they both decided was better than McQuaid's), and making inroads into the Sam Thompson (an altogether superior drink!). An assortment of whiskeys, mostly Irish, had been sent across by Willie Mourne.

An understanding had developed between them over the last two days – a liking even – which meant they could canter along together in total silence without feeling they had to make conversation. Neither had anything to say on the way to a funeral – a mass affair. Both were full of their own thoughts.

Danvers was pretty pleased with the way he had handled the whole business. He'd kept the two witnesses apart, Betty under armed guard at home, Lannen in the gaolhouse, so they couldn't teamwork their stories. And by this simple device he'd helped to satisfy himself they were both on the level.

He'd sure given it a mighty turning over in his head, conscious that he was more or less the judge and jury if it didn't go to court. Eventually, he'd decided there were pretty weighty reasons for believing them. His trip to the old Marriott place, had, indeed, been lost trouble, the Darling Gang being about as much in evidence as Ulysses S. Grant. He couldn't fail to see how Casey had hornswoggled him and, hell he'd never liked the boy, never trusted him, was well rid.

Then there was Betty Barnes, a sweet-natured lass if ever he'd seen one. She sure wasn't the type to see her pappy gunned down and then lie about the circumstances. And Willie Mourne had been able to confirm many of the details. Last but not least to be chewed over was Major Thomas Lannen's distinguished war record and his reputation for honesty.

'Course it might have been different if folks had been clamouring for a hanging, but nobody was, not even Hender's or Barnes's own men. Seems like neither of the deceased was mighty popular with anyone.

They dismounted and walked up to the large gathering. He saw Lannen slip away awkwardly, and knew where he was heading. It was no surprise to him to see the farmer take the girl's arm.

Somebody had to support her, he reckoned.

* * *

After it was all over, they rode back together, Lannen and Betty. He was the first to speak when they were well away from the throng, deliberately wandering from the track, across the hard-knuckled range.

'Betty, how you bin?'

When words came to her, they came as a flood. 'I've been out of my mind with worry for you,' she said. 'They told me you might be strung up. I didn't know what was happening. They wouldn't tell me. I suppose they didn't know. Maybe they were trying to frighten me into confessing something. I kept telling them the truth, the way it happened. I guess they must have believed me.'

High above them in the darkening sky, which held a metallic tint, were five circling black buzzards. Then came a serpentine lash of blue lightning that hung about the horizon, far away but near enough to scatter the heavy birds. The two horses were fretful and skittish, especially when their riders dismounted, rather than spurring homeward.

'If I didn't know better,' he said, holding the flat of his hand out, 'I'd say it's gonna ... rain.'

Suddenly, thunder crashed all about them. 'I don't believe it,' she said. 'Not after all this time.'

He took her gently in his arms and held her closely as the first light drops began to descend. 'When it starts, it's sure gonna go on for weeks and months,' he said. 'Folks like us is gonna have to stay indoors.'

'Your place or mine?' she said.

'Oh yours. Yours is kinda dandified and fit for a lady like you to live in.'

'I'm gonna need a bossman to look after it,' she said archly, tossing back her mane of black hair on which heavier drops were falling. 'Somebody strong....' He winced as she flexed his bad arm. 'Somebody quite strong,' she murmured as though to herself. 'Somebody I can trust. Someone like you.'

The rumble of thunder had become almost continuous now, like a drumbeat, and the rain brought down a thin dark veil across the sky. 'You offerin' me a job, ma'am?'

'Well somebody's gotta work on our land,' she said.

'Your land?'

'Our land, yours and mine – and maybe Hender's if we can raise the capital.'

'I sure got me enough for a big down payment,' he mused. 'I reckon we could get it.'

Though the rain was intensifying all the time, cascading down them, bouncing off in huge blobs the size of tears, the thirsty yellow earth was swallowing it all up without trace. They stood there, arms about each other, shielding their eyes against it, hunching their shoulders the rain was bruising through their clothes.

'So I got the job?' he asked, uplifting his face to

hers and starting to unstring the sodden black bodice that was clinging to her.

'Yeah I reckon you'll do.' Mechanically , she had started to pull at the buckle of his belt and he breathed in to assist.

'And what kind of wages you payin'?'

'Aw, that's business,' she said, holding a finger to the water channelling down his nose, then raising her face, eyes tightly closed, to the stinging cleansing balm. 'I'll leave all that for you to work out.'

'And what you gonna be doin'?' he asked, pulling her down gently, so she was astride him on the still-dry earth.

'Why for the next ten years at least, I'm gonna be all tied up ... havin' your babies!'

'I want a son,' he said, without a moment's hesitation.

'I want plenty of them and a few girls besides. D'you reckon you can support all that lot?'

'Yeah, I reckon so. I'm gonna be one of them there Texas cattle kings!'

'Herefords?' She screwed up her face.

He studied her expression and wondered if they were about to have their first difference of opinion. Then he smiled wickedly. 'Uh, right now, I kinda got a fancy for ... the longhorn!'

She widened her eyes and looked incredibly beautiful.